"They're going to look

"Who?" Cash asked.

"The cops," Carlyle answered. "The significant other's the first person suspected."

"I haven't been Chessa's significant other for a decade."

"Doesn't matter. The ex with custody of their kid? Primo suspect."

"No one will think I killed my own daughter's mother."

"You can list the reasons people shouldn't suspect you, but you're the ex-husband."

"I didn't kill anyone."

"I know that. But do you have an alibi? You're on their list, and once they have a time of death, they're going to want to know where you were."

"I trust the cops, Carlyle."

"You shouldn't. They're not gods. They're just people. We need to look into it ourselves, and you need an ironclad alibi."

"Look, I appreciate the advice. But I know I didn't do it. There can't be any proof I did. I'm just keeping my head down and making sure Izzy's okay."

"She's never going to thank you for martyring yourself for her. She'll probably blame herself for it."

"Speaking from experience again?"

COLD CASE
PROTECTION

NICOLE HELM

Harlequin
INTRIGUE

For the dogs we miss.

ISBN-13: 978-1-335-45710-3

Cold Case Protection

Recycling programs for this product may not exist in your area.

Harlequin Enterprises ULC
22 Adelaide St. West, 41st Floor
Toronto, Ontario M5H 4E3, Canada
www.Harlequin.com

Printed in U.S.A.

Nicole Helm grew up with her nose in a book and the dream of one day becoming a writer. Luckily, after a few failed career choices, she gets to follow that dream—writing down-to-earth contemporary romance and romantic suspense. From farmers to cowboys, Midwest to *the* West, Nicole writes stories about people finding themselves and finding love in the process. She lives in Missouri with her husband and two sons, and dreams of someday owning a barn.

Books by Nicole Helm

Harlequin Intrigue

Hudson Sibling Solutions

Cold Case Kidnapping
Cold Case Identity
Cold Case Investigation
Cold Case Protection

Covert Cowboy Soldiers

The Lost Hart Triplet
Small Town Vanishing
One Night Standoff
Shot in the Dark
Casing the Copycat
Clandestine Baby

Visit the Author Profile page at Harlequin.com.

CAST OF CHARACTERS

Cash Hudson—The middle Hudson sibling. Keeps his distance from the Hudson Sibling Solutions work and focuses on training dogs.

Izzy Hudson—Cash's twelve-year-old daughter.

Carlyle Daniels—Works for Cash. Her brother married into the Hudson family, so she lives on Hudson Ranch.

Walker and Mary Daniels—Carlyle's brother and Cash's sister. They are married.

Anna and Hawk Steele—Cash's sister and her husband, who's an arson investigator.

Palmer Hudson and Louisa O'Brien, and Grant Hudson and Dahlia Easton—Hudson brothers and their girlfriends.

Jack Hudson—Oldest Hudson brother. Head of Hudson Sibling Solutions and also the sheriff of Sunrise, Wyoming.

Detective Laurel Delaney-Carson—Detective at Bent County investigating the kidnapping attempt and then murder.

Chessa Scott—Cash's ex-wife and Izzy's mother.

Chapter One

Carlyle Daniels had grown up in a tight-knit family. Dysfunctional, trauma-bonded—no doubt—but close. She supposed that's why she loved being absorbed into the Hudson
clan. Their tight-knit was familiar, but bigger—because
there were so many more of them.

So, yeah, a few more overprotective males in the mix, but
she had *sisters* now—both honorary and in-law, because her
oldest brother, Walker, had married Mary Hudson last fall.

Carlyle liked to talk a big game. She *really* liked to
tease her oldest brother about how lame it was he'd gotten
old and settled down, but deep down she could not have
been happier for him. After spending most of his adult life
trying to keep *her* safe while they tried to figure out who
killed their mother, he now got to settle into just…normal.
He worked as a cold case investigator for Hudson Sibling
Solutions and helped out on the Hudson Ranch and was
going to be a *dad* in a few months.

Her heart nearly burst from all the happy. Not that she
admitted that to anyone.

She'd been working as Cash Hudson's assistant at his
dog-training business on the ranch for almost a year now.
She'd settled into life on the Hudson Ranch and in Sunrise,
Wyoming. It was still weird to stay put, to not always have

to look over her shoulder, to know she just got to…make a life, but she was handling it.

What she was not handling so well was a very inappropriate crush on her boss—who was also her sister-in-law's brother, which meant she probably *shouldn't* ever fantasize about kissing him.

But she did. Far too often. And normally she was an act-first-and-think-later type of woman, but there were two problems with that. First, she no longer got to bail if she didn't like her circumstances. She was building a life and all that, and bailing would bum Walker out which just felt mean and ungrateful.

Second, Cash had a daughter, who Carlyle adored. Izzy Hudson was twelve, smart as a whip, sweet and funny. She also had a little flash of something Carlyle recognized. Carlyle didn't know how to explain it, but she knew Cash didn't see it. She didn't think any of Izzy's family saw it, because the girl didn't *want* them to see it.

Carlyle saw through Izzy's masks all too well. She'd been the same all those years ago, keeping secrets so big and so well, her brothers hadn't found out until last year. So, she felt honor bound to keep an eye on the girl, because no doubt one of these days she was going to run headfirst into trouble.

Carlyle knew the lifelong bruises that could come from that, so she wanted to be…well, if not the thing that stopped the girl, the cushion to any catastrophic falls. She considered herself something of a been-there-done-that guardian angel.

Carlyle looked up from the obstacle course she'd been setting up for the level-one dogs and surveyed her work. She was satisfied and knew Cash would be too. He hadn't been super excited about hiring her. The fact he'd even done it had been because Mary had insisted or persuaded him to—but Carlyle knew that was more about him being a control freak than anything *against* her.

She liked to think she'd proved herself the past year—as a hard worker, as someone he could trust. She glanced over at the cabin that was Cash and Izzy's residence, while everyone else lived up in the main house. Palmer and Louisa were just a few weeks out from a wedding and finishing up their house on the other end of the property, but everyone else seemed content to stay in the main house. It was certainly big enough.

Carlyle sometimes felt like the odd man out. She wanted to be like Zeke, her other brother, and have her own place in town, but staying on the property made a lot more sense for what her work schedule was like.

And for keeping an eye on Izzy.

Who, speak of the devil, stepped out of the front door of her cabin, followed by her father and then Copper, one of the dogs retired from cold case and search and rescue work.

Carlyle sighed, in spite of herself. There was something *really* detrimental to a woman's sense when watching a man be good with animals and a really good dad whose top priority, always, was his daughter's safety.

Or maybe that was just her daddy issues. Considering her fathers—both the one she'd thought was hers, and the one who'd actually been hers—had tried to kill her. More than once.

But Don, the fake dad, was dead. Connor, the real dad, was in jail for the rest of his life. So, no dads. Just brothers who'd acted *like* fathers.

And now, for the first time in her life, safety. A place to stay. A place to put down roots. She had not just her brothers, but a whole network of people to belong to.

Copper pranced up to her and she crouched to pet his soft, silky face. "There's a boy," she murmured.

She glanced up as Cash and Izzy approached. Cash was a tall, dark mountain of a guy. All broad shoulders and cowboy swagger—down to the cowboy hat on his head and the boots on his feet. His dark eyes studied her in a way she had yet to figure out. Not assessing, exactly, but certainly not with the ease or warmth with which he looked at his family.

And still, it made silly little butterflies camp out in her stomach. She felt the heat of a blush warming her cheeks like she was some giggly, virginal teenager when she decidedly was *not*.

She was a hard-hearted, whirling dervish of a woman who'd grown up fast and hard and had somehow survived. Survival had led her here.

Things were good. She was happy. She wouldn't ruin that by throwing herself at Cash, and she wouldn't ruin it by failing at this job or messing up being part of this family network.

No, for the first time in her life, Carlyle was going to do things right.

CARLYLE DANIELS WAS a problem. Worse, Cash Hudson couldn't even admit that to *anyone* in his life. She was a good worker, Izzy *loved* her, the animals *loved* her and she was an even better assistant than he'd imagined she'd be.

But he found himself thinking about her way too much, long before he'd stepped out of the cabin this morning to see her across the yard getting work for the day set up.

He too often found himself trying to make her laugh, because she didn't do it often enough and the sound made him smile…which he also knew *he* didn't do enough. As his siblings and daughter routinely told him so.

But if anyone had *any* clue he smiled more around Carlyle than he did around anyone other than Izzy, he'd be flayed alive.

He was too old for her—in years and experience. He was a father, and he had one disastrous marriage under his belt. He could look back and give himself a break—he'd been sixteen, reckless enough to get his high school girlfriend pregnant, and foolish enough to think marriage would make everything okay.

Maybe he was older, wiser, more mature these days, but that didn't mean he could ever be *good* for anyone. Didn't mean he'd ever risk Izzy's feelings again when she already had oceans of hurt over the mother she hadn't gotten to choose.

He wasn't even interested in Carlyle. He just thought she was hot and all the settling down going on around the Hudson Ranch was getting to him. Grant and Mary were fine enough. They were calm, settle-down-type people. Mary might be younger than him, but he'd always figured her for the marriage-and-kids type—and even if he liked to play disapproving older brother, Walker Daniels was about as besotted with Mary as a brother could want for his sister.

Grant was older, far more serious, and he and Dahlia had taken what felt like forever to finally even get engaged, so that was all well and good. Cash could take all those little blows that reminded him time marched on.

But it was Palmer and Anna who *really* got to him. Younger than him. The reckless ones. The wild ones. He'd never have pinned Palmer for marriage, and he'd never thought anyone would want to put up with the tornado that was Anna.

But Palmer was getting married in a few weeks, and by all accounts Louisa was the answer to any wildness inside of him. Anna was a *mother* now, and a damn good one, and somehow she'd found a man who thought all her sharp edges were just the thing to shackle him down forever.

Someday, sooner than he'd ever want, Izzy would be an adult. Making her own choices like his siblings were doing. Izzy would go off into that dangerous world and *then what*?

Cash pushed out an irritated breath. Well, there was always Jack. Single forever, likely, being that he was the oldest and Cash couldn't remember the last time he'd been on a date, or even gone out for a night of fun.

They could be two old men bemoaning the future and the world together.

And no one would ever know he had an uncomfortable *thing* for Carlyle. He blew out a breath before they finally approached the obstacle course. "Morning," he offered gruffly.

"Good morning," she said brightly, grinning at Izzy as she stood up from petting Copper.

"I'm going to walk Izzy over to the main house, then we'll get started."

"Dad," Izzy groaned, making the simple word about ten syllables long. "I can walk to the house by myself. It's *right there*." She pointed at the house in question. Yes, within his sight, but…

Too much had happened. Too much *could* happen. As long as his ex-wife was out there, Izzy wouldn't leave his side, unless she was with one of his family members.

"I'll be right back," he said to Carlyle.

Izzy didn't groan or grumble any more. He supposed she was too used to it. Or knew he wasn't going to bend. He wished he could. He wished he could give her everything she wanted, but there'd been too many close calls.

They climbed up the porch to the main house in silence and he opened the back door that led into a mudroom.

"I'm not a baby," Izzy grumbled. Probably since she knew he would follow her right into the house until he found someone to keep an eye on her.

He didn't say what he wanted to. *You're* my *baby.* "I know, and I'm sorry." They walked into the dining room, and Mary was already situated at the table with her big agenda book and a couple different colored pens.

She looked up as they entered and smiled at Izzy.

Cash would never not feel guilty that Izzy ended up with such a terrible mom, but Mary as an aunt was the next best thing, he knew.

"I'm craving cookies. What do you think? Should we make chocolate chip or peanut butter?"

Izzy didn't smile at her aunt, she just gave Cash a kind of killing look and then sighed. "What do you think the baby wants?" She went over and took the seat next to Mary at the table.

Mary slung an arm around Izzy's shoulders, and Izzy leaned in, putting a hand over Mary's little bump.

Izzy didn't want to be treated like a baby, she didn't want him being so overprotective, but she also loved her family. She was excited about cousins after being the only kid on the ranch for so long, and she *liked* spending time with her aunts and uncles.

So this wasn't a punishment. He tried to remind himself of that as he retraced his steps back to where Carlyle was waiting. She'd brought out the level-one dogs, and they were lined up waiting for their orders.

Because they were level one, there was still some tail wagging, some whining, some irregular lining up, but they were good dogs getting close to moving to level two. They all kept their gazes trained on Carlyle, and she stood there looking like some kind of queen of dogs. Her long, dark ponytail dancing in the wind, chin slightly raised, gray-blue eyes surveying her kingdom of furry subjects.

He came to stand next to her and didn't say anything at first. Ignored the way his chest got a little tight when she glanced his way, like he was part of that array of subjects she ruled.

She could, he had no doubt. If he was someone else in a totally different situation, she no doubt would.

"She's tough," Carlyle said, not bothering to explain she was talking about Izzy.

As if he didn't know that about his daughter. As if he hadn't raised her to be tough. As if life hadn't forced her to be. "Yeah, and the world is mean."

"Take it from someone who's been there and done that, it doesn't matter how well-intentioned the protection is, at a certain point, it just chafes."

Cash knew she wasn't wrong, but it didn't matter. "I'd rather a little chafing than any of the other alternatives."

Carlyle sighed, but she didn't argue with him. She surveyed the lineup of dogs. "Well, you want to start or should I?"

Carlyle was good at this. A natural. "Take them through the whole thing."

She raised an eyebrow. He hadn't let her do that before all on her own, but…it was time. He couldn't give his daughter the space she needed to *breathe*, so he might as well unclench here where it didn't matter so much. "You can do it."

She grinned at him, eyes dancing with a mischief that was far too inviting, and completely not allowed in his life.

"I know," she said, then turned to the dogs and took them through the training course. Perfectly. A natural.

A *problem*.

Chapter Two

Carlyle had never been a good sleeper in the best of times. She wouldn't admit it to anybody, but she preferred to sleep with the lights on. The dark freaked her out when she was alone. Too many shadows. Too many unknowns.

But she'd learned that first night at the Hudson house that living with too many people meant they noticed. A light under the door at all hours, or when they woke up before her and walked by her window outside, off to do their chores. Then there were questions.

So, she dealt with the dark the best she could. She focused on how safe the Hudson ranch was. Due to the nature of solving cold cases, and the danger they'd seen over the past year, they had all kinds of security systems and surveillance.

Besides, the man who wanted her dead was safe behind maximum security prison-bars. But a lifetime's worth of running—because even before her mother had been murdered they'd been on the run—meant she had a hard time shaking fear loose.

Tonight was no different. Lately, she'd been sort of letting fantasies of Cash lull her off to sleep, but she was beginning to think that wasn't very healthy. She'd gone to the Lariat last night—the local bar—with Chloe Brink, one of

Jack's deputies at Sunrise Sheriff's Department, and three different men had hit on her.

She hadn't been the slightest bit interested. Worse than all that, Chloe had called her out on it.

Uh oh. You've got the look.

What's the look?

The look of a woman hung up on a Hudson who is perennially in the dark.

Carlyle wasn't sure she'd felt that embarrassed since Walker had tried to give her a sex talk when she'd been fourteen.

So, which one is it? Chloe had asked, like it was just a foregone conclusion she was hung up on a Hudson. *A single one, I hope.*

Oh my God, yes. Which was an admission, and she couldn't believe she'd been stupid enough to fall for such an easy ploy.

Chloe had grinned. *Doesn't leave too many of them these days. Cash is more age appropriate.*

Does that make Jack more age appropriate for you? Carlyle had retorted. Getting too bent out of shape about the truth, but not being able to stop herself.

Chloe had looked at her bottle with a hard kind of unreadable stare. *Jack is my boss.*

Cash is my *boss.*

Chloe had finished off her one and only beer, because she was driving. *Maybe we've both got issues.* Which had made Carlyle snort out a laugh.

Then Chloe had driven her back to the ranch and idled outside the big house, staring at it with an opaque expression. She'd sighed, a world's worth of knowing in her voice. *They'll mess you up, Car. If I were you, I'd steer clear.*

Carlyle hadn't known what to say to that. Chloe was the first friend she'd made outside of the Hudson ranch, and she didn't want to be a jerk. She liked the feeling of having someone to go to who didn't revolve around *family*. Like she was a normal, functioning adult who had not just a strong family life, but friends. Interests. Things outside this sprawling ranch.

Maybe a boyfriend who was *not* her boss.

She decided then and there she was not going to fantasize about Cash to fall asleep anymore. She would think about the dogs. About work. About Izzy.

But all those things just circled back to Cash.

Eventually, she got irritated enough with herself that she slid out of bed. She went over to the armchair next to the window. She sat down on it and rested her arms on the windowsill and looked out at the great, vast night around Hudson Ranch.

The stars sparkled above. This place was so beautiful. She'd grown up jumping from city to city, but she was certain— deep in her bones—she'd been made for *this*. Mountains and sky and fresh air.

She knew her brother Zeke didn't feel comfortable taking too much from the Hudsons, but Carlyle liked to think they'd earned it with the way they'd grown up. Why not enjoy the generosity of people who could spare it?

Not that the Hudsons had seen only sunshine and roses. Their parents had disappeared when they'd been kids, and only the determined, taciturn dedication of their oldest brother, Jack, had kept the family together.

But they'd had this ranch, they'd had money and the community of Sunrise. They'd even built their own cold case investigation company. All Carlyle had ever had since her mother had been murdered was Walker and Zeke.

She'd damn well enjoy a nice house and pretty surroundings now no matter how they came along.

Except just as she was thinking it, like some kind of grand cosmic joke, the security light kept on at all hours—since the trouble last year—went out. Just one moment it was on, the next it wasn't.

She frowned. It was supposed to stay on all night. Still, the landscape was well lit by the moon and stars and... Was that a shadow over by Cash's cabin?

"You're being ridiculous," she whispered to herself. "Paranoid." But she pressed closer to the window, squinting in the dark. It was probably a dog. Or a bear.

But it looked damn human. And the security light had gone off.

"Don't overreact," she whispered to herself again. She went back to her bed and reached for the lamp. She'd spend the next hour or so reading or something. She turned the switch.

Nothing happened.

She sucked in a shaky breath, let it out. *Coincidence.* The bulb had just burned out at an inopportune time. Something normal. Boring. If she went around waking everyone up and screaming, she would look panic-addled. They'd all start treating her with kid gloves, like she was some kind of victim.

When she was a *survivor.* She swallowed and moved over to the switch by the door. She flipped the switch.

Once again, nothing happened.

She flipped it again. Once, twice. Three times.

The lights wouldn't go on. Terror swept through her. Not an accident. Not a figment of her overactive imagination. But it could be a perfectly innocent loss of power, she tried to remind herself over the panic. Even though it wasn't storming. Even though this had never happened the whole time she'd been living here.

She rushed back over to the window, hoping she'd look out into the night and not see a thing.

But *something* was moving around Cash's cabin in the moonlight. No power shouldn't matter when it came to the security systems. They should have a backup, but...

Maybe it was nothing. Maybe the security system would catch it. So many maybes.

She couldn't just stay here and do nothing. She thought about texting Cash, but again... If it was nothing, she couldn't stand looking like she didn't have a handle on everything she'd been through.

She strode over to her closet and keyed in the code for the gun safe she kept on the top shelf. She pulled out her gun and then left her room. She considered knocking on Jack's bedroom door since it was the only other bedroom on the main floor, but no. It would be too embarrassing to be wrong with any of these people.

Besides, she had a gun. She knew how to use it. She knew how to handle danger. So, she'd handle this on her own because it was *nothing*, and no one would have to know she'd overreacted.

It was fine. She'd check it out, make *sure* it was fine, then wake someone up about the power outage. Once she was sure there was no other danger.

She unlocked the side door and slid out without making a sound. She looked up to where she knew a camera was situated. They were motion activated and should have moved with her. Even in the dark.

They didn't.

Power outage. Backup outage. It was...fine. It had to be.

She moved off the porch and toward Cash's cabin, led by moonlight and a spiraling fear that made it hard to breathe evenly. But the closer she got, the more she could see the outline of a shadow. At the side of the house. The side she knew Izzy's room was on. She wanted it to be a dog, but when no growls or barks broke out, she knew it couldn't be true.

Carlyle crept closer. Her heart was thundering in her chest, but she'd been in positions like this before. Once she was close enough, she cocked her gun.

"Freeze," she ordered sharply.

The shadow stopped. It turned toward her. He or she was standing right next to the window to Izzy's room. The window was open a crack, a little light shining on the other side of that curtain. Izzy's night-light no doubt.

Oh God. Carlyle should have called someone. Said something. She should have trusted her gut. When had she stopped doing that?

"If you don't tell me who you are in two seconds, I'm going to shoot," Carlyle said. Luckily, a life of danger meant that even though her insides shook and terror had taken hold, she sounded cool and in charge.

But the figure didn't speak. Carlyle heard the soft sound of a growl from inside. No doubt Copper. Hopefully alerting Cash or Izzy that there was trouble.

Still the figure didn't speak.

Carlyle raised her voice, held the gun steady. "Okay then. One—"

A high, piercing scream tore through the world around them. Then raucous barking followed.

Izzy. Copper. Cash.

But they were inside. Was someone in there with them? Was someone hurting Izzy in the cabin? What would have happened to Cash if that was the case?

So focused on thoughts of Izzy and Cash, Carlyle forgot about the present danger and turned toward the cabin.

The blow was so hard, it seemed to rattle her bones and

she lost her footing, her balance. She fell onto the hard, cold ground, the blow now burning. Like she'd been…stabbed in the process?

But the hard sound of footsteps retreating meant whoever had been there was running away. They'd never spoken.

But…the scream. Someone was inside with Izzy. Carlyle had to get… She tried to get up, but the pain about took her out. She rolled over onto her stomach, tried to get to her hands and knees. She managed, but only just barely. She had to grit her teeth against the pain, and the fuzzy light-headedness that wanted to take over.

She heard the slam of a door, footsteps. Copper ran up to her first and licked her face, whimpering. "Thanks, bud," she muttered. She looked beyond the dog to the other foot-steps.

Cash. Barefoot, hair haphazard, gun in one hand and flashlight in the other. But he was standing and whole.

"Carlyle," he said, clearly with nothing but confusion.

"They got away." Had she lost consciousness? "Izzy?"

"I'm okay," came the girl's wavering voice. She was hud-dled behind Cash, holding on to him for dear life.

"Cops are on their way," Cash said as he approached. "What the hell happened?" He swept the flashlight over her head, then down her shoulders.

"I saw someone outside Izzy's window. I…"

"Daddy, she's bleeding."

Cash swore, immediately kneeling at Carlyle's side. "Come on." Then he lifted her up into his arms.

IT WAS TOO dark to walk her across the yard to the main house safely. Someone had been out here and gotten away, so he couldn't risk Izzy out in the open.

"Hold the door open for me, Iz."

She scrambled to do just that as Cash carried Carlyle to the cabin porch. "You still with me?" he asked through gritted teeth as he maneuvered her into the dark entryway.

"I'm okay. Really. They just knocked into me. I think I hit my head."

That would explain the blood, hopefully. Head wounds usually bled more than was necessary. It needed to be… something like that. He needed to get a good look at her though, see for himself. He laid her down on the couch in the living room as Izzy flipped on the lights. He didn't need to tell Izzy to lock all the doors or stay close. She was too used to this.

He wanted to swear again, but he kept it inside his head. He studied Carlyle's face, saw no traces of blood. "Where'd you hit your head?"

"Uh…" She reached up, patted around. "I guess I didn't. I'm okay."

But there'd been blood. He frowned at her. What the hell was she… His thoughts trailed off as his gaze tracked down her shirt. There on her side, her shirt was all bloody…and the blood was soaking into his couch.

This time he did swear, and Izzy didn't even scold him. "Why didn't you tell me?" he demanded, reaching forward to lift her shirt.

Carlyle's eyes darted behind him as she grabbed his wrist to stop him from lifting up her shirt.

She was looking worriedly at Izzy. She was trying to protect Izzy. "It's okay. Really. Got any Band-Aids?" She tried to laugh, but it clearly hurt because she squeezed her eyes shut.

She was going to need *stitches*, not a Band-Aid, with that amount of blood. Cash didn't know how to sort through every terrible emotion battering him. She was injured, Izzy was terrified. Hell, *he* was terrified, but he wanted Izzy out of earshot before he asked Carlyle what happened.

A knock sounded at the door, and even though Cash knew bad guys didn't *knock*, he grabbed onto Izzy before she could rush to answer.

"Who is it?" he called out.

"Jack."

Since he recognized his brother's voice, he let Izzy go. "Go ahead."

Izzy scrambled for the front door and let Jack in. Jack locked the door behind him and then strode forward.

"Grant, Hawk and Palmer are checking the perimeter. Anna's trying to figure out what happened to the security system. Fill me in," he demanded, all sheriff even though he was in pajamas. He held his gun in one hand, cell in the other.

Cash looked at Carlyle. Her worried gaze was on Izzy. Something twisted in his gut, sharp and complicated, but he pushed it away. Had to focus on the task at hand.

"Iz?" he forced himself to say. "Can you go grab a washcloth and some bandages? Some of the antibiotic ointment. We'll get Carlyle all fixed up." Which was a lie, but it would get Izzy out of earshot for a minute or two.

She nodded and ran for the hallway.

Cash looked at Jack, kept his voice low. "Carlyle needs to go to the hospital."

"The 911 call should pull in an ambulance. If not, one of my deputies will run her there on code. Let's try to sort out what happened so she can go straight there."

"I couldn't sleep," Carlyle said. And she *sounded* alert and with it. Maybe the bleeding wasn't so bad.

"I was just sitting in my room, looking at the stars out the window, and the security light went off." She swallowed. "At first, I thought…it was just nothing. Then the lights didn't work. I thought I saw a shadow so I…came to check it out."

"Without telling anyone?"

"Yeah, without telling anyone," she replied, not bitterly exactly, but certainly with some acid in her tone. "That shadow could have been anything, including a figment of my imagination."

"But it wasn't," Cash said. Because Izzy had screamed. He'd rushed to her bedroom to find Copper growling at the window and Izzy cowering in the corner.

"I don't have any great details," Carlyle continued. "It was all shadows. There was someone by Izzy's window. I had my gun, so I told them to stop. Tell me who they were. But then Izzy screamed, and Copper went nuts inside and I… I got distracted. So the person rushed me." She looked down at the bloody shirt. "I guess stabbed me too."

Jack nodded, no doubt filing away all the information. And his brothers and brother-in-law checking the perimeter would look for prints. Any evidence of whoever had been here.

But someone had been right outside his daughter's window, and he hadn't even *known*. He'd come to rely on those security cameras and look where it had led him.

Izzy rushed back in with the first aid kit and a dripping washcloth. Cash took them from her and then maneuvered her so she was facing Jack, not Carlyle and her bloody shirt.

Jack knelt in front of Izzy, put his hand on her shoulder. "What made you scream?"

She swallowed and Cash was overwhelmed with the guilt of how little he'd been able to protect her from danger. She was only twelve and she'd already seen far too much for a grown woman, let alone a middle schooler. He'd tried to shelter her from so much and failed. Every single time.

Cash lifted up Carlyle's shirt. The bloody gash on her side, just above her hip—where an intricate and colorful tattoo wound around pale skin—would definitely need stitches, and that was probably his fault too. He pressed the washcloth to it, then put her shirt back down. He took her hand and pressed it on the shirt over the lump of washcloth. "Can you hold it?"

She nodded as Izzy began to answer Jack's question.

"Copper was growling," she said. "It woke me up. I was getting out of bed to get you, Dad. But then… I heard a weird noise. It took me a minute to figure out it was someone opening my window. Then I heard voices and I just… screamed."

"What kind of voices, honey?" Jack asked, rubbing a hand up and down her arm.

"I heard someone say *stop*." She looked over her shoulder at Carlyle. "You, right?"

Carlyle nodded.

"Then I heard this kind of…creepy breathing. Right by my window. Copper was really growling now and I… I didn't know what else to do."

"You did good," Carlyle said firmly.

Izzy's bottom lip wobbled before she steadied it. "You're hurt."

Carlyle shrugged. "I'm fine."

A pounding started at the door. Not police yet, from the sounds of it. Carlyle's expression went grim. "You better let him in before he tears the door down with his bare hands."

Jack sighed and got up, unlocked the door and opened it for one of Carlyle's brothers.

Walker was barefoot. Hair wild. Eyes hot and angry.

Yeah, Cash couldn't blame him. He'd be looking the same if situations were reversed.

"What the hell is going…" His gaze landed on Carlyle on the couch, and even though she was holding pressure on the wound, the blood was visible on her shirt and the couch. Walker started to swear as he crossed the room to her.

"Come on, Walker," she said firmly, even though she was too pale and this was taking too damn long. "Not in front of the kid."

Walker came up short as if finally realizing there were other people in the room, one of them a twelve-year-old girl. He blinked once at Izzy, then his expression went blank. "Someone explain to me what's happening."

"No big deal. Just got a little knocked around when I found someone outside Izzy's window. Cops are on the way."

"An ambulance too, I hope."

"It's okay. She's going to be okay. She said so," Izzy said, sounding very close to tears.

Cash pulled her into him, gave her a squeeze. "She's going to be just fine, but we'll have a doctor check her out just in case."

"Hopefully he'll be cute," Carlyle said, making Walker groan.

But it also did what it was supposed to do, Cash supposed. Izzy didn't look *quite* so distraught. Walker didn't look *quite* so murderous. She'd lightened the tone, made them think that because she could crack a joke all was well.

The door opened behind Walker, this time Hawk. "Didn't find anything," he said, his expression cool and blank. "Cops are coming up the drive. Why don't we move up to the main house for questioning. They're going to want to search around the cabin anyway."

"I'm going to take Carlyle to the damn hospital myself," Walker said.

"Barefoot?" Carlyle replied with a raised eyebrow. "Going to toss me in your truck too?"

Her brother scowled deeply, but by that time a police cruiser had parked outside the cabin. Then it became the usual. The far too usual. Cops and an EMT and moving to the main house while Carlyle and Walker went to the hospital.

There were questions, so many questions, and an exhausted Izzy curled up on his lap because she was afraid. Terrified. So terrified that he didn't even bother to bundle her up into one of the guest rooms upstairs. He just sat on the couch and let her sleep in his lap long after everyone had gone or retreated back to bed.

Like she was a baby again. He brushed a hand over her tangled hair. "I'm sorry I haven't done a better job, baby," he muttered. Like he had so many times over the years. No matter how hard he tried, he couldn't seem to give her the life she deserved.

The police had no answers, but Jack was down at the sheriff's department to find out what he could. They'd all work together to figure it out, to get answers, to protect Izzy. But Cash was so tired of this…constant battle. Every time he eased into some new season of his life, something like this happened.

Sometime before dawn, he heard light footsteps and looked up to see Anna enter the room, carrying a fussy Caroline. Anna sank into the rocking chair across from the couch where he sat, Izzy asleep across his lap.

Cash had a very vivid memory of being sick one winter not long after Anna had been born, sleeping on this couch, and waking up to his mother in the same position with baby Anna.

Now Anna was the mother, and he hadn't seen his own for half his life. Time just kept inching on.

"The obvious answer is Chessa," Anna whispered, her expression hot and mean even as she snuggled Caroline to her chest. Anna and Chessa hadn't gotten along even when Cash had still been married to Izzy's mother.

"Maybe," Cash said. He knew she was talking about who was outside Izzy's window overnight, but it didn't sit right. Chessa was tiny. Granted, when she was high she could inflict some damage, but it was hard to believe she could do the damage done to Carlyle.

An even bigger stretch was Chessa having the know-how to cut the electricity. She might know the ranch well enough, but she wouldn't know how to tamper with the generator and make sure all the security system batteries were dead *along* with cutting the electricity.

"Not on her own. No, but who else would be after Izzy?" Anna demanded.

"I don't know," Cash muttered, looking down at his sleeping daughter. But they needed an answer this time.

A final one.

Chapter Three

Carlyle was bitter about the stitches. She hated needles and hospitals and know-it-all doctors even when they *were* cute.

She was bitter about Walker hulking about like some kind of overprotective dad when she was *fine*. "Go home to your wife."

"I'm going to have the doctor check you for brain damage."

She rolled her eyes. This lousy hospital bed was uncomfortable, and the IV in her arm was making her want to crawl out of her skin. Made worse when Walker finally stopped *pacing* and sat down on the hospital bed next to her.

"What were you doing out there, Car?"

"Checking out a threat."

"Why didn't you come get me?"

"I'm not a kid. You gotta get that through your head. I wasn't going to wake you and your pregnant wife up when I wasn't even sure it *was* a threat."

"You should have. Or called Cash. Or grabbed Jack. Literally an entire ranch full of people who would have helped at your fingertips, and you walk out into the dark alone. Everything could have gone so much worse."

Carlyle looked hard out the window. Day had risen. Cars came and went from the parking lot. She had to blink back tears. It could have been so much worse, but this was bad enough because if she'd had backup, maybe whoever it was wouldn't have gotten away.

"I feel guilty enough, thanks."

He sighed and patted her IV-less arm. "I'm not trying to make you feel guilty."

"Doing a hell of a job anyway."

"Whether or not they track down who it was, you stopped something from happening to that little girl, Carlyle."

"The police don't have anything, do they?"

"Not yet. Mary's updating me as she hears, but we won't know what Jack's found until he's done."

"It just means she's going to keep being in danger."

"And she's got an army of people protecting her, Car. It's not the same. All you had was us."

She hated that he could see through her so easily, that he might be feeling his own guilt. "You two were pretty top notch."

"Not like the Hudsons."

No, they hadn't had a ranch or a community or much of anything the Hudsons offered Izzy. A sheriff as an uncle among them.

"We did the best with what we had. Not exactly your fault."

"Nah." He squeezed her hand. "But the things we blame ourselves for don't have to be our actual fault to feel like we should have made a different choice. But there's no different choice. There's only the one you make in the moment, and then how you learn from it. Don't go it alone, Car. Not anymore. None of us needs to."

"This feels like a pep talk for our brother."

"Yeah, but he's not chained to a hospital bed, so he just leaves when I try."

"I know it's not my fault," she said, both because it was

true and because he needed to hear her say it. "I know it worked out that I happened to look out there when someone was sneaking around." Or maybe if she didn't *know* it, she tried to convince herself of it. "It had to be her mom, right?"

"That's what most of them think."

"Most?"

"According to Mary, Cash isn't totally sold, at least on it just being her. Doesn't think the mom has it in her to orchestrate that kind of attack on her own."

Carlyle frowned at that. It *was* pretty orchestrated. It was a lot for one person to handle, because it wasn't just cutting the security light and the electricity, it was debilitating all the security backups and getting to Izzy all in a short period of time. But *why*?

"We'll get to the bottom of it," Walker said. "And more, we'll all protect Izzy. She's lucky she's got so many people who've got her back."

But it wasn't luck to be a little girl who felt like a target. Carlyle should know. Luckily, the doctor came in, because she didn't know how to convince Walker she was fine, or that she didn't feel guilt, or that she was going to magically not worry about Izzy no matter how many people were looking after her.

It took another couple hours, mostly of waiting until she wanted to scream, before they finally released her and Walker drove her back to Hudson Ranch. Walker walked her right to her room—no detours allowed. Mary was waiting there for her, and it was clear she'd tidied up Carlyle's room, changed the sheets, had a tray of snacks waiting.

"I don't want to be fussed over," Carlyle grumbled as she got into her bed, hating that it was a lie. She absolutely wanted pillows fluffed and snacks delivered and Mary's soft, easy presence. She was so perfect, and Carlyle might have hated her for it if Mary didn't love Walker so much, if she wasn't going to make the best mom to Carlyle's future niece or nephew.

"Oh, dear," Mary said, sounding truly perplexed. "You sure got messed up with the wrong family, then." She arranged the tray on the nightstand and shot Carlyle a grin.

Carlyle wanted to keep pouting, but it was too hard. Mary really did embody that old saying about glowing while pregnant. And Walker sliding his arm around her waist and looking down at her like she hung the moon only added to it.

It was everything she wanted for her brother, but if she thought too much about it, the lack of sleep and pain medicine would likely make her cry and she didn't want to indulge in that just yet.

"You know, a girl who's been stabbed deserves to know the gender of her first niece or nephew."

Mary looked up at Walker, who gave a nod. "It's a boy," Mary said, her smile soft and wide.

Carlyle hadn't expected Mary to actually answer. She really hadn't. It made her want to cry all over again.

Luckily, Izzy popped her head in the doorway. Mary moved out of the way to let Izzy in. "Can you keep an eye on her for me, Izzy? I've got some brownies in the oven I need to check on and Walker has some work to do."

Izzy nodded solemnly, and when they left the room Izzy produced a little clutch of wildflowers she'd clearly picked and tied together with a pretty little ribbon. She walked over to where Carlyle sat on the bed and held them out.

"Do you like them?"

"I *love* them." Carlyle took the outstretched flowers and a took a deep sniff of the blooms, then patted the space on the bed next to her. "Hop up. I'm not fragile."

Izzy was studying her with big, worried eyes, but eventually she crawled up onto the other side of the bed. Carlyle lifted her shirt high enough so Izzy could see the small bandage over her stitches.

"See? It's nothing."

Izzy reached out and touched the edge of the bandage, then Carlyle's tattoo, her mouth all pursed together in a frown. "My friend's aunt got shot in the leg. It was a long time ago, but it still hurts her sometimes."

"My God, what's in the water around here?"

That *almost* made Izzy smile. She cocked her head. "What's your tattoo of?"

Carlyle dropped her shirt. She didn't think Cash seemed like the type of person who'd be thrilled with his daughter getting a tour of Carlyle's tattoos. She had a few, all easily hidden by normal clothes.

Izzy sighed at Carlyle's lack of response, but she didn't push it. "I know this has something to do with my mother. I don't know why she… I don't know. But I'm sorry that—"

Carlyle pulled her as close as she could without causing too much physical pain under the weird numbness of pain meds. "Listen." *Life's a bitch and then you die* was on the tip of her tongue, but Cash probably wouldn't like that one piece of advice, even if it was borderline suitable for a twelve-year-old. "I don't do sorrys. Because I don't do anything I don't want. So no one's gotta be sorry when I wade in, because I did it because I wanted to."

"But—"

"No buts. Them's the breaks, kid. Now, I went through some scary stuff when I was your age too. And it's not that different. My mom was okay, and I had some pretty good older brothers, but my dad sucked. Hard. The kind that put us all in danger. So, I know how it feels. I do."

Izzy didn't say anything, just looked down at her hands

in her lap. But slowly, ever so slowly, she leaned her head on Carlyle's shoulder.

Carlyle might have lost it right there, but she knew she had to be strong for Izzy. "It makes you feel helpless, but… It's a good lesson. You can't control anyone but yourself. So you focus on being the best version of yourself you can be. And sometimes you go through hard stuff that makes you wonder *why*, but then…there's all this."

Carlyle pointed out the window. Izzy's eyebrows drew together as if she didn't understand what Carlyle meant.

"I've been holding my own for the past two years because I wanted some space from my brothers. I was alone, and I was lonely. And scared. It was hard to get through that, but now I get to be here. Horses. Dogs. I'm going to be an aunt. And you're going to be a cousin. That's pretty cool."

Izzy nodded after a while. "I like babies. Caroline cries a lot, but she's so cute."

"Yeah. I'm not saying you don't get to be scared or unhappy because you've got an awesome family and place to live, but what I want you to understand, accept, *know* is that everyone in this place will do whatever they can to keep you safe, and that's nothing to be sorry about. Even though sometimes it doesn't feel like it, that's a gift. We'll all keep you safe. That doesn't mean you're weak, or a burden. Because you've got some responsibility too. You were going to get your dad. You screamed. You did the right things."

"Maybe," Izzy said, but she was clearly not fully buying it. "Can I ask you a favor?"

"Anything."

She lifted her head, turned those big blue eyes on Carlyle. "I want to learn how to shoot a gun, Carlyle. And you're the only one who'll teach me."

Ahh… Hell.

LITERALLY LESS THAN forty-eight hours after she'd been *stabbed*, Carlyle was in the dog pens, being a pain in his ass.

"You aren't working," Cash said. Ordered. "Go back to the house."

"If I don't have something to do, I'm going to lose my mind."

"Take up knitting."

"I'd rather bleed out, thanks."

He laughed in spite of himself. Which was bad because she grinned at him and wouldn't take him seriously now.

"The doctor said no heavy lifting," she continued. "But the nurse said I should keep mobile. I don't want to get all stiff and weak over a few stitches. Besides, I needed to talk to you about something away from Izzy. Work seemed about the only option."

Cash frowned. He didn't like the sound of that. At all. Particularly when Carlyle looked...nervous.

"How do you feel about Izzy and... Look. She came and talked to me yesterday... The thing is..."

"Spit it out, Carlyle," he snapped, because he couldn't begin to fathom what this was that would have Carlyle, of all people, stumbling over her words. About *his* daughter.

"She wants me to teach her how to shoot a gun."

Cash barked out a laugh, and not a nice one. "She knows that's not happening. I've told her she has to wait until she's sixteen. And I don't appreciate her trying to talk you into going against that very clear rule. I'm going to go over there right now and— "

Carlyle grabbed him, held him in place. "You can't tell her I told you. She'll never tell me anything again."

"Good! She shouldn't be telling *you* anything anyway."

Her head drew back like he'd slapped her, and it took him a second, but he got it. Too late, but he got it.

"I didn't mean it like that."

She stepped away from him and crossed her arms over her chest, her expression cool and detached. Trying to hide the hurt. "Oh, yeah? How did you mean it?"

He blew out a long breath. *This* was why he'd kept their lives somewhat isolated. *This* was why he hadn't wanted an assistant. Why he and Izzy lived in their own space.

He was in charge of his daughter, and he didn't do well with anyone butting in telling him how to do that.

Now he had to somehow apologize to Carlyle for something he *hadn't* meant, while making it clear she could in no way get involved in this decision regarding his daughter.

"You don't understand." He shoved a hand through his hair, trying to find the words. "How hard this…" He blew out a breath. Maybe he didn't have the right words, but he had a very clear truth. "My daughter *loves* you, straight through."

Carlyle looked at him with that expression she very rarely showed. It was a little too vulnerable for her usual badass bravado. And it weakened his defenses against her, because he knew better than most that soft spots and hurts lived under a tough exterior.

"I love her too," Carlyle said, very quietly. Seriously.

"Yeah. I know. I do…know that. Hell, Car, you've got a stab wound to prove it. But she came to you on this because she knows I'll say no. She wants it to be a secret. I can't accept that. I won't, not with all this going on. Secrets between us aren't safe, and I know she hates it, but sometimes you hate the things people do to protect you."

Carlyle swallowed visibly. But she nodded. "I'm not going to do it against your wishes. If I was going to do that, I wouldn't have told you in the first place. Just let me… Let me try to make it her idea to tell you, okay? I'll try to convince her to tell you before we do anything, but you can't go storming in there yelling at her that she can't. She's *scared*, Cash. And she has every right to want to do something about it."

"Nothing is happening to her."

"No, nothing is. I know you're scared too. We *all* are. But she's a kid who feels like everything is happening *to* her. Why wait four years? What's that going to change? I know you have to be the worried, careful dad. I get that, I really do. But you don't get how it feels to be that kid. You're an adult who gets to feel like you have some kind of control."

"You think I feel like I have *any* kind of control?" he shot back. He hadn't felt in control of a damn thing since his parents disappeared when he was fourteen.

Carlyle crossed over to him, put her hand on his arm. "But when we're adults, we get to *do* stuff about that feeling. You can't expect her to just sit there and be protected. Trust me, Cash. I know your family has been through some bad stuff, and no doubt Jack did annoying things to try to protect you, but it's got nothing on being the youngest kid in a group full of people who think they know what's best."

He tried to take that on board because it was true. Carlyle had been more in Izzy's shoes than he ever had been. Maybe he'd felt like his entire adult life had been about rolling with a hundred different punches, but he supposed Carlyle was right. He could punch back whenever he wanted, and he was always telling Izzy to let him handle it.

"I don't like the idea of her dealing with guns. Not at this age. Maybe I'm wrong, but that was always the family rule. Unless you wanted to go hunting, no guns until sixteen."

"Can't you make a compromise for special life circumstances? Can't you at least teach her how to *shoot* one, even if you don't want her to have access to a firearm?"

"What'd be the point of that?"

"Knowledge, Cash. Knowing how to do stuff makes you feel like you can…handle things. I don't know how else to explain it. Knowledge is power."

Cash didn't know how to take that fully on board. It wasn't that he thought she was wrong. Worse, it felt like she was right. And all the ways he'd tried to protect Izzy from things—from her knowing bad things, understanding awful things—might have been the wrong choice.

"She's the most important person in the world to me. I just want to protect her."

"I know." Carlyle swallowed, like this was hard for *her*. "I think I know better than most. And while I can't know how you are feeling as a parent, I have been in her situation. I know what she needs, Cash. I know what it's like to know someone out there is after you, and it doesn't matter. I had the two best brothers in the world protecting me, but it didn't *matter*. I kept secrets I shouldn't have, secrets that got my brother shot, and put all of us, including you guys, in danger. I just… If I can help her and you not go through that, I will stick my nose where it doesn't belong. Sorry."

Her hand was still on his arm, and he understood that she was trying to *help*. He had so much help, so much support in his family, but Carlyle really was the only one who had a kind of insight into what it felt like to be in Izzy's position. Cash had never really thought of that before.

He patted her hand. "I appreciate it, even when I don't."

She laughed at that, her mouth curving and her blue-gray eyes taking on that little sparkle of mischief that was so much *her*. "I guess it helps I don't mind ticking people off."

"You?" he replied, with mock surprise, which made her laugh again.

There was something about the sound of it. Like a magnet. He always found himself moving closer. Getting a little lost in that dimple in her cheek.

Someone behind him cleared their throat and Carlyle jumped while Cash dropped his hand from over hers, like they'd been caught doing something other than *talking about his daughter.*

"Sorry to interrupt," Jack said as Cash turned to face him.

"Not interrupting," Cash muttered, shoving his hands into his pockets. He would have felt embarrassed, or worried what Jack thought, if he hadn't recognized that blank, cop look on his brother's face. Bad news. Cash moved forward. "What is it? Iz—"

"It isn't about Izzy," Jack said, quick and concise. "She's at the house and is fine."

"Then what is it?"

"Bent County found Chessa."

"Good." Cash knew it wouldn't be that simple, but it was a start. "Are you going to go question her or are they? I'd like you to be there. I'd…"

Jack let out a breath. Stepped forward. Bad news, all around, Cash could feel it. Like Mom and Dad all over again. Jack reached out, put a hand on his shoulder. "She's dead, Cash."

Cash had no idea how to absorb that. But that wasn't all.

"It's looking like murder."

Chapter Four

Carlyle knew she couldn't possibly feel as shocked as Cash, but it was close. Dead. Murder. A kidnapping attempt that now made even less sense.

And the two Hudson brothers, standing there *so* still. Jack's hand on Cash's shoulder and Cash barely even taking a breath.

"I don't understand," he finally said, his voice little more than a scrape. "She...she was murdered?"

"That's the premise they're operating under. I'm still working on getting more details out of Bent County. It's an ongoing investigation and they know I've got personal ties, so I'm getting shut out. I sent Chloe over to the coroner's office to see if she could get something for us to go on. But I have a bad feeling this will work its way through the town grapevine, so I wanted to tell you before you got exaggerated word of it from someone else."

Carlyle had an uncomfortable, vivid flashback of Walker telling her what had happened when she'd been at school that she...she had to look away, take a few steps back.

This wasn't about her. This wasn't...the past. Not her mother murdered all because Carlyle had been tired of moving around, had thrown a fit because she wanted to stay in one place.

It was just the horrible roll of the dice that scattered similar tragedies around the world. And how her mother had dealt with the man who'd wanted her dead was hardly Carlyle's fault, no matter how often she felt like it was.

"I have to tell Izzy," Cash said, his voice still that awful, pained gasp of a man drowning.

"You could wait," Jack said. "Give us some time to find more answers. She's not leaving the ranch, so it's not like she'll have contact with anyone running their mouth. Let's take some time to get all the information."

"She'll know." Carlyle knew she should have kept her mouth shut, this wasn't her family, her business. But she… Even more so now, she had been in Izzy's shoes. Her mother had been murdered when she'd been a kid. And Carlyle had *loved* her mother, depended on her for everything, blamed herself for her death, so it was different. It was so different.

But right now, it felt the same. It was too many commonalities, and too much understanding Izzy's position to keep her mouth shut. She retraced her steps to stand next to Cash again, to face off against Jack.

"She won't know if no one tells her," Jack said, a clear warning in his hard tone.

Carlyle should nod and agree because this wasn't her family or her business, and it'd be smart to heed Jack's warning. But… She turned to Cash. "It doesn't matter how careful you all are. If *you* know something *she* doesn't, that's this big and this important, she'll feel it. And she'll worry it's about what happened at the cabin. She'll make it into something else, she will feel…like an outsider. Trust me, when you feel like that, you make bad choices."

Cash turned to look at her, but every move seemed weighed down. Like he was swimming through molasses. In his head, it probably felt like it.

"What do you mean, Carlyle?" he asked, with the weight of the world on his shoulders.

She wished she could heft some of the load. "I just mean…" She looked from Cash to Jack then back again because Cash was clearly the only receptive audience. "My mother was murdered too, you know. When I was Izzy's age. Walker and Zeke… They tried to shelter me, keep the sordid details from me, but the thing was, I already was too deep in. I knew secrets, but they tried to keep me separate. I know it was to protect me. I know they were trying to do the right thing, the *good* thing, but it put us at cross purposes. We spent too many years…" She trailed off. She didn't need to go down the full tangent of her life. "I know this isn't the same situation. You aren't Walker and I'm not Izzy, but I just know what it's like to be in her position. You feel powerless, and you'll do some pretty reckless things to find some power. Especially if everyone you love is keeping something from you."

"*You* felt that way," Jack pointed out.

Carlyle tried not to scowl at him, but hiding her frustration with him was a hard-won thing. She managed not to scowl, but her tone was snappish when she spoke. "Yeah. You got a lot of experience being a twelve-year-old girl whose mother was murdered?"

Jack, predictably, said nothing in response. That was the problem with all this childhood trauma bred into the very fabric of this ranch. They thought because they'd had it rough, they understood all the layers of what was rough for anyone else.

But Carlyle could see, very clearly, there was something very different about losing your parents suddenly and without knowing what really happened, and knowing that someone had *killed* one of them, on purpose, for you to find.

The Hudsons looked at Izzy and saw their own problems, but even Carlyle couldn't begin to guess what the little girl felt about the terrible mother she'd barely known—by all accounts—being murdered.

What Carlyle *did* understand was being the little girl left out of the discussion, someone not *part* of what was going on.

"I know you guys had stuff too," Carlyle said, her focus on Cash because he's who she had to convince. He had the final say in his daughter's life. "I can't imagine what it's like to have your parents disappear into thin air, but it's not the same." Of course, Carlyle couldn't resist a *little* dig. "You were in charge, Jack. She's not. And she knows it."

Jack's scowl was epic. He crossed his impressive arms over his chest, all tall and glowering and intimidating.

Too bad Carlyle had grown up at the feet of intimidating. She didn't so much as *blink* at him.

"You know I'm right," she said to Cash. "I think you have to know I'm right."

Cash didn't look at her. He looked at some spot on the ground. Making Carlyle realize this wasn't *just* about Izzy. Maybe this Chessa was his *ex*-wife, maybe he didn't love her anymore, but he'd married her once. Had a kid.

He'd lost something too.

Sympathy swept through her, and she reached out to touch his arm or something, but he chose that moment to move forward. "I'm going to go tell her," Cash muttered, pushing past Jack.

Leaving Carlyle to face off against a clearly very disapproving Jack. Which she should have left alone, but disapproving authority had never sat well with her, no matter how well-meaning.

"You don't have to agree with him or me, Jack. She's not my kid and she's not your kid."

"They're all mine," he muttered, but he didn't argue anymore, just turned and strode away as Cash had.

Leaving Carlyle alone with the dogs. Her side throbbing, her heart aching and far too many memories making it all too easy to worry about what Izzy might do next.

But the one thing she was reminded of quite plainly by Jack's parting words hurt just as much.

None of them were *hers*.

CASH WENT FOR whiskey that night. He rarely drank anymore. At most, a beer here or there. Never hard liquor. Never with Izzy under the same roof. It tended to remind him a little too much of the hell he'd raised when he was far too young.

It was hard to remember that kid. He was nothing like the boy who'd lost his parents—angry and confused and scared, but too much of a fourteen-year-old to admit it. So he'd caused trouble, fought with Jack, drank, ran with the wrong crowd.

Everything had changed at seventeen when Izzy had been born. So tiny. So *his*. A responsibility he owed to everyone in his life to see through. To take more seriously than any other responsibility he'd ever been gifted. He'd given up everything wild in that moment.

Chessa had never felt that. At the core of all their marital issues, that was number one. Everything in Cash's life had changed when Izzy had taken her first breath, and Chessa had wanted nothing to change. Cash hadn't struggled to give up their wild, reckless ways. Chessa had always been desperate for one more hit.

Now Chessa was dead. He'd always known she was heading in that direction. Too much drinking. Drugs. Getting mixed up with dangerous people all for a hit. He'd felt at turns guilty about it, and at turns—which made the guilt nearly swamp him now—wished she'd just get it over with so he wouldn't have to worry about her hurting Izzy anymore.

She'd lost the ability to hurt him a long time ago, if she'd ever had it to begin with.

A sad state of affairs, through and through.

Now he'd had to tell his daughter her mother was dead. At someone else's hand. He'd planned on just telling her Chessa had died, leave the details out of it, but Carlyle's words had haunted him.

So he'd told Izzy the truth. A slightly sanitized version of what little he knew, but definitely the important parts.

Izzy hadn't cried. She'd been upset, he knew. She hadn't tried to hide the hurt. But it was more fear and confusion.

And definitely hiding something. He wouldn't have seen it if Carlyle hadn't brought up her own experiences, but she was right. Trying to protect Izzy had only led him to this place where his little girl didn't trust him with everything.

He let out a long breath. Why not get really drunk? There were a hundred people in this house to take care of things, and as long as no one fully knew what had happened with Chessa, and the kidnapping attempt, Izzy would be sleeping at the big house. More eyes, more bodies, more protection.

But not more answers.

The storm door squeaked open and Carlyle slid out into the dark, one of his dogs trailing after her. Copper would be up in Izzy's room, but Swiftie—who should be sleeping out at the dog barn—had clearly latched on to Carlyle.

Both woman and dog surveyed him, then Carlyle jutted her chin at the porch chair. "Mind if I join you?"

"Would it matter if I did mind?"

Her mouth curved at that, and she went over and settled herself next to him on the porch swing rather than the open chair. Swiftie settled under her feet.

He didn't scowl, but he wanted to.

"I don't want to butt in," she began.

He snorted. "Don't you?"

She sighed, then grabbed his drink—right out of his hand—and took a deep swig like it was a shot. *Hers* for the taking.

"Are you even old enough to drink?" Because he liked to remind himself—when he was feeling a little too bruised and bloody and tempted to lean on her—that she was over five years younger than him, and he had no business wanting her company.

She gave him a killing look. "It wouldn't matter to me if I was, but I'm not *that* young, Cash. In fact, I'll be twenty-four next month." She handed the glass back to him.

He grunted. "I had a seven-year-old by the time I was twenty-four."

"And I had put a famous and powerful senator in jail by the time I was twenty-three. Want to keep playing this game?"

She really was something else. Everything inside him felt too heavy to allow a laugh to escape, but she made him *almost* want to.

"I'm too tired, and not drunk enough, to play any games."

"Well, if I were you, I wouldn't go down the drunk route. I know how this goes. I can't tell if Jack knows and is sparing you, or if he's in denial because you're all upstanding Hudsons. They're going to look at you first."

"Who?"

She turned to him then, her gray-blue eyes as serious as her expression in the dim light of the repaired security pole. *Some security.*

"The cops. When someone is murdered, the significant other is the first person they start digging into."

"I haven't been Chessa's significant other for a decade. I haven't even had contact with her in close to five years. The few times she's come sniffing around, someone else dealt with her."

"Doesn't matter. The *ex* with custody of their kid? Especially a kid who's been a target? Primo suspect."

"No one who knows me is going to think I killed my own daughter's mother. No one with any sense is going to think I waited all these years to do it, either. Why now? I *do* have custody. I have everything. Chessa was the one with nothing." Because of her own choices, he had to remind himself.

"Jack isn't investigating. Bent County is. And even if he was, even if someone who 'knows you' was, they shouldn't."

"Why the hell not?"

"Because he's your *brother*. Because personal connection is a red flag, Cash. You want people thinking you did it? You want to be a true crime podcast in ten years so people can look at Izzy and wonder? You can list all the reasons people shouldn't suspect you, but all anyone is going to see is that you're the ex-husband."

If he sat with what she was saying, he understood. If he could detach himself from the situation, he'd probably agree with her.

But they were talking about *him*. And Izzy. And Chessa. And murder.

"I didn't kill anyone."

"Well, I know that. But do you have a good enough alibi? Was that weird kidnapping attempt some kind of...decoy?

You gotta start thinking with that investigator brain of yours, because the cops are slow and wrong half the time."

"I'm not an investigator anymore."

"You try to stay out of it for Izzy. I get that and I haven't been around that long. But I also see how much you *want* to be involved. You've got the skills. If not by use, by osmosis. And lucky for you, I've got the knowledge of how this goes down. You're on their list of suspects, and once they have a time of death, they're going to want to know where you were."

Sometimes, she made no sense and yet he felt like she saw right through him all at the same time.

"I happen to trust the cops, Carlyle."

"You shouldn't. They're not gods, Cash. Not saying they're bad or evil. They're just people. Human, capable of error and getting drowned in too much red tape. And if I'm trusting just people, it's going to be the people I know and love who don't have to worry about paperwork. We need to look into it ourselves, and *you* need an ironclad alibi."

He wanted to beat his head against a wall, but that wouldn't change anything. If there was one thing he understood in this life, it was that the blows never stopped coming, no matter how many you'd already had.

"Look, I appreciate the advice. Maybe you're not even wrong. I don't know. But I know I didn't do it. There can't be any proof I did, because I didn't. I'm just going to keep my head down and make sure Izzy's okay. No investigating around the cops, no worrying about alibis. Just her well-being."

Carlyle paused for a very long time, abnormally still and looking out at the twinkling night with a serious expression on her face when she was usually a whirl of excess energy and movement.

When she finally spoke, it was quietly and seriously. "She's never going to thank you for martyring yourself for her. She's going to wonder why her dad didn't have a life." She took another long sip of his drink. "And then probably blame herself for it."

She looked a little miserable, which was unfair since she was telling him *he* was about to be a prime suspect for murder. "Speaking from experience again?"

"Yeah. I had to kick Walker out of my life so he'd go live his." She turned, flashed that smile that always looked a little dangerous, but in this light he saw it for what it was. Deflection. "Look at him now. Married. About to be a dad. I did that, and has he thanked me?"

Cash could see the similarities between him and Walker whether he wanted to or not. Between Carlyle and Izzy. But… "I get it. You lived this weird version of what she's going through, but you're not the same." He took the glass from her, finished off the drink. Not enough to get drunk, but she was probably right about that being a bad idea.

"No. No two people are the same. Maybe it's different when it's your dad giving up everything he enjoys for you. But you've walked a little in our shoes too, Cash. Don't you ever worry about Jack and all he's given up to keep you guys going?"

He wanted to swear, because of course he worried about that. Because it was true. Jack had sacrificed a million times over, to keep them together, to keep the ranch going, to start Hudson Sibling Solutions. And on and on it went.

Cash looked at the empty glass in his hands. He knew he shouldn't say any more. Shouldn't prolong whatever this was. A pep talk or advice or whatever. But he felt like the words…had to be said. She was the only safe place to say them.

It was the strangest realization, in this already strange moment, that he didn't really *have* much of a safe place. Not when he was so busy trying to protect his daughter, his siblings, himself.

He didn't need to do that with Carlyle. "I used to wish she was dead. I just thought it'd be easier."

She was quiet, but only for a second or two. Then she put her hand on his shoulder, much like Jack had earlier today when he'd delivered the news.

But Carlyle's slim hand felt different than his brother's. Like comfort without the strings of who they were. Because she was right about too many things. And she understood these…strange, twisted, tenuous trauma-laden relationships.

"I don't blame you, Cash. I doubt you're the only person in your family to feel the same. Izzy included. But don't tell it to the cops. My bet? They'll be sniffing around first thing in the morning. Have an alibi. Even if you have to lie."

"Why would I lie?"

"Because if the murder happened some night you and Izzy were sleeping in the cabin out there, that's not enough of an alibi. They'll ask you to prove you didn't sneak out and do it and sneak back."

"With Izzy sleeping *alone*?"

Carlyle shrugged. "She's twelve, Cash. Not an infant. And *I* know you wouldn't leave her alone. Anyone here knows you wouldn't, but that doesn't mean much to cops looking for someone to lay the blame on. You have to be smart about this. Izzy needs you to be smart about this. Sometimes being smart means bending the truth a bit. You've got this big mess of a family behind you, and you're innocent, so that helps, but you can't let it make you complacent."

He studied her. So serious and earnest, which was not her usual MO. "Which one of them sent you out to pep talk me?"

She frowned quizzically, as if she didn't understand what he meant at first. Then she looked at the house, and something in her expression changed again. But he couldn't read it.

But he got the feeling it meant *no one* had sent her out. She had come out all on her own. Wanting to offer him advice to protect himself.

He didn't know what to do with that.

She got up off the swing. "I'm your guardian angel, obviously." She flashed that mischievous grin, but it didn't land. She was making a joke out of it because she was uncomfortable.

And since she was, he played a long. "Angel? Hardly."

"I am *reformed.*"

He snorted, but he got to his feet too. She moved for the door, but he reached out, got ahold of her hand to stop her. He gave it a squeeze.

"Thanks. I do appreciate the butting in, even when I don't like it. Because Izzy is the most important thing. I'll listen to anyone if I think it'll keep her safe. So butt in, be annoying. If it's for her benefit, I'll deal."

She looked down at their hands, but she didn't pull away or act like she was uncomfortable. He couldn't see her expression, but they just stood there on his family's porch holding hands.

Which suddenly made *him* feel uncomfortable, because it felt like all those intimate connections he'd spent years avoiding. Shrank his world down to not feel anything that didn't involve his family. Because shrinking down was *safe*, and he had to be safe. For Izzy. No matter what Carlyle said.

He dropped her hand, and she looked up. But she didn't quite meet his gaze.

"Any time," she said breezily, grabbing the storm door and opening it. Swiftie trailed behind her as she stepped inside and away from him.

He watched them disappear inside and wondered why it felt like a mistake.

Chapter Five

Carlyle shook out her hand as she walked back to her room. Not the time or place to get all...*whatever* over a little hand-holding. Over actually helping someone, instead of always being the one who had to be helped.

Cash thought she was young, and wrong.

But he'd listened to her. Thanked her. Squeezed her hand like what she had offered meant something. It did a hell of a number on that pointless soft heart of hers she was always trying to bury.

She opened her bedroom door. "You, Carlyle Daniels, are a grade A—" Before she could finish insulting herself, she stopped short. Froze.

Izzy was sitting in the middle of Carlyle's bed. Crying.

What Carlyle wanted to do was cross the room and gather Izzy up in her arms and tell the little girl she would literally fight every last demon to the death if she stopped crying.

But that was what no one—men in particular—ever understood. Sometimes, it wasn't about someone fighting the battles *for* you. Sometimes, it was about feeling you had the power to fight them yourself.

So Carlyle did her best to take her time, to tack on a smile. To give Izzy a little space at first.

"Hey. What are you doing in here? Pretty sure your dad

will have a meltdown if he goes to check in on you and
you're not in bed." Carlyle moved to the bed and took a seat
on the edge.

Izzy sniffled, wiping her nose with her sleeve of her pajamas. "I've got ten more minutes. He's like clockwork."

Oof. How well she knew these little games. The way
some kids observed too much, filed far too much away. All
to hopefully never be caught off guard again.

But the off guard always came.

Carlyle gently laid her hand on Izzy's shoulder. Much
like she had with Cash outside. Two hurting people, so determined to hurt *away* from each other, rather than show
each other their vulnerable underbellies.

Oof times a million.

"I know you're scared. You've got every right to be right
now. And you're probably tired of hearing it, but it's true.
No one's going to hurt you, Izzy. You are the most protected
girl in Wyoming. I'm working on convincing your dad to
let you learn how to shoot. Because you should feel like you
can protect yourself too, but he's gotta be on board with it.
You've both got to be honest with each other."

But Izzy was shaking her head before Carlyle even finished. "I'm not worried about protecting *me*," Izzy said, like
Carlyle was crazy. "I don't want anyone to hurt my dad."

Carlyle felt a bit like she'd been stabbed all over again.
But she tried not to let it show. "Why would anyone hurt
your dad? Look, I realize I'm relatively new to the situation,
but it sounds like Chessa was mixed up in some dangerous stuff. Stuff your dad wouldn't touch with a million-
foot pole."

Izzy's expression was stubborn. Her eyes were shiny
and puffy, but she'd stopped actively crying. "I don't think
someone tries to get me one night, and Chessa shows up

two days later dead, and it doesn't connect. It *has* to connect. I'm worried it connects to my dad, not me."

She sounded so adult. So like her father. But she brought up an interesting and terrifying point. With Chessa out of the way, what did anyone want with Izzy? What had Chessa even wanted with Izzy if, by all accounts, she hadn't wanted to be a mother?

Didn't that mean Cash might be the *actual* target? What better way to get to him than through the daughter he cherished and protected above all else?

Carlyle studied the girl, trying to find a good place for her whirling thoughts to land. There were still tears in Izzy's eyes, but underneath was a quick mind that caught on. That understood.

No matter how little her family wanted her to.

"The two things might not connect," Carlyle offered, even though she didn't know how that would possibly be true. "Maybe it's just bad timing Chessa was murdered."

"Maybe," Izzy agreed, still reminding Carlyle a bit too much of Cash right then. The careful, measured way she didn't *argue* with what Carlyle had said, but was clearly internally working through all the ways she didn't agree.

And she was going to keep those thoughts bottled up and to herself, because she didn't think the adults listened. Carlyle squeezed her shoulder. "So, how *could* it connect? What do you think?"

Izzy blinked. Once. Then looked down at her hands. "No one cares what I think," she muttered.

"First of all, I know that isn't true. You all care about each other more than just about anybody. But I think all that care, mixed up with danger, tends to a lot of…isolating yourselves and keeping secrets. You're here, in my room, crying, because you don't want your dad to see you're upset, right?"

"I know it hurts his feelings when I cry. I know… He's like the *best* dad. I do know that. I don't think he does."

Stab me in the heart, kid. "I mean, maybe you could tell him. Or not keep secrets from him."

She watched the mutinous expression begin to storm across Izzy's face and quickly changed tactics.

"Tell me how you think it connects, Izzy. Let's see what we can figure out."

The girl frowned. "Well, it's not the first time my mom tried to take me, right? If it *was* my mom who hurt you."

Carlyle hadn't heard the whole story of that, but there'd been rumblings from the Hudson contingent about an incident a while back.

"Last year," Izzy continued. "She helped that guy who tried to hurt Aunt Anna and shot Uncle Hawk? She told Uncle Hawk that she…" Izzy curled her hand into the bedspread. "She wanted to sell me or something. I don't really get that, but everyone was pretty upset about it."

Carlyle felt like she couldn't *breathe*. Sell… What an absolutely awful thing. Surely…

"No one told you about it?" Izzy asked, clearly reading Carlyle's shock.

Carlyle shook her head, unable to find her voice. Sell your own kid? Hell, her biological father had tried to have her killed, so she shouldn't be surprised at how terrible parents could be, but…

"They didn't tell me either, but I heard them talking. I always hear them talking, no matter how sneaky they think they're being." She picked at the bedspread. "But Aunt Anna and Uncle Hawk and Dad and everybody stopped that whole thing. They outsmarted the guy. Well, mostly. He shot Uncle Hawk."

Carlyle was struggling to come up with words. She'd always thought she had it pretty rough, but this girl had seen her damn share.

Izzy looked up at Carlyle earnestly. "That guy was mad because Hudson Sibling Solutions hadn't found his son alive. He wanted like revenge or something. So, what if all this is like…revenge? My mother didn't like Dad or our family. Maybe someone else didn't either. Maybe someone doesn't want to hurt *me*. They want to hurt my dad. Take me. Murder my mother. I don't know how *that* would hurt him, but maybe someone thought it would because she was my mother."

Carlyle could think of a reason someone would murder Chessa to hurt Cash. If they were going to have him take the fall.

But as much as she was all about the truth and not keeping secrets, Izzy didn't need to know that. Not yet.

"That's possible," she agreed, though it killed her to put that look of worry in the girl's eyes. "But right now, it's just as possible as anything else. Do you…know anyone who'd want to hurt your dad?"

"I know my mother hated him. Hated all of us. So maybe someone who knew her?"

"Not a bad thread to tug." But someone who had a relationship with Chessa probably hadn't killed her. Probably. But if the Hudsons had enemies… "I'll look into it."

"Really?"

"Really. And if you think of anyone, or anything that seems fishy—not just lately but even years ago—you tell me. We'll see if we can put it all together."

"We?" Izzy asked suspiciously.

"Look, I'm not going to go behind your dad's back. I'm

not going to lie to him. The way I see it, you all need to do better at working together. Not separately."

"He won't listen. He'll just keep hiding me away. Telling me to stay safe and stay out of it."

"Maybe," Carlyle agreed equitably. "But he'll be wrong to do it, and I'll tell him so. We're going to work together on this one. All of us. I'll see to it." Because Izzy's thought process was a good one, and maybe they didn't need to terrify her with all the possibilities, but she had to feel like she wasn't just someone to be hidden away.

Izzy studied her with big, serious blue eyes. Carlyle didn't know what to do with the intense gaze, so she just… took it.

"I don't want anything to happen to him, Carlyle," Izzy said, her voice little more than a whisper. "Even when I'm mad, I…"

"Listen…" She figured if it worked for the father, why not for the daughter? "You don't have to worry about your dad. I'm going to look after him. I'm going to be his guardian angel." Then she couldn't resist it anymore. She pulled Izzy into a tight hug. "I swear, Iz. I'll keep him safe." *Both of you.* "Whatever I have to do."

She'd keep that promise, no matter what it took.

CARLYLE HAD BEEN RIGHT. First thing in the morning, two Bent County detectives were waiting in the living room before Cash had even gotten his coffee. He sidestepped them and took the back way into the kitchen before they saw him.

He needed to prepare himself.

Mary was already looking fresh and neat per usual, had coffee mercifully brewing, and a whole breakfast spread on its way.

"Don't you ever have morning sickness?"

"Why do you think I'm up this early? Wakes me up before the sun, but then when the sun comes up, I'm *starving*." She nodded toward the front of the house. "They want to talk to all of us, but you first. I told them to wait," Mary said, frowning over the tray of breakfast foods she was putting together. "And suggested that the next time they wanted to do some questioning they should maybe call first. Or appear at a decent hour."

"Did they point out they're trying to solve a murder?"

Mary puffed out a breath. "Regardless. That's no excuse for bad manners."

"It probably is exactly the excuse for that."

Mary clearly did not agree, but she was not an arguer. "Take your time. Drink your coffee in here. I'll keep them busy until you're ready."

"I'll never be ready," Cash muttered. How did a person answer questions about their ex-wife's murder? His daughter's awful mother? He studied Mary, Carlyle's words from last night haunting him now that she'd been right about the cops' appearance.

"Carlyle's worried about my alibi."

Mary stopped what she was doing, looked at him, a slightly arrested expression on her face. "Walker said the same thing."

"Did you tell him the police know what they're doing, and I'm innocent so he's overreacting?"

Mary blinked. "Well. Yes."

"Yeah. I'm starting to wonder if we're *underreacting*."

"We have security footage," Mary said, her umbrage fully in place. "That will prove that you were here and—"

"Yeah, about that?" Palmer said, also coming into the kitchen through the back way. No doubt avoiding the cops too. "We don't have security footage."

"What?" Mary and Cash demanded in unison.

"I was up all night dealing with the security network. I figured the cops would want proof of where we all were, and that's easy enough, right?" Palmer poured himself a big mug of coffee. "It's all been wiped. Everything before the kidnapping attempt. It looks like some kind of...reset put in motion by the backup batteries failing, and maybe it is, but the timing is suspect."

Cash set his coffee down. This was...bad. Really, really bad.

"If Chessa was killed *after* the night Carlyle got stabbed, we've got all the footage we need. But..."

"It's going to be before," Cash finished for him.

"You don't know that," Mary insisted.

But he did. In his bones. Coincidences didn't just *happen*. Not like this.

"Just tell the truth," Mary said, even with worry etched into every inch of her expression. "You don't have anything to hide."

"Yeah," Cash agreed. He didn't have anything to hide, but he couldn't help but wonder if Carlyle would be right yet again. He took the mug of coffee. "Might as well get this over with," he grumbled, then he pushed off the counter and headed for the living room.

He knew the male detective. Thomas Hart was with Bent County and had worked on a few of their cases last year. He didn't know the blonde woman.

"Hart," he greeted. "Mary said you have some questions for me?"

They both stood up, and Thomas gestured toward the woman. "My partner, Detective Delaney-Carson."

"Ma'am."

She nodded and shook his hand, then they sat.

The woman took the lead. "A lot of this is just procedure. Outlining the players. Trying to get a sense of who might have seen Ms. Scott alive last."

Cash nodded. "I can guarantee you it wasn't me. I haven't actually seen her in years."

"There was a report from last year and the year before that she was on your property."

"The first time, she dealt with Anna and only Anna as far as I know. Second time, she was involved in the kidnapping and attempted murder, if I recall correctly, of Hawk Steele. All dealt with by other members of my family and the Sunrise Sheriff's Department."

"Where your brother is sheriff?" she asked lightly.

But it wasn't a question.

The detective made some notes on a pad of paper. Then continued to ask the usual inquiries. What was their relationship like? Non-existent. How did he feel about Chessa's lack of mothering? Ticked off but philosophical considering he didn't want Izzy around her when she was high. What did he know about Chessa's drug use and on and on.

But Cash *was* too much of an investigator at heart, even if he tried not to be. They were asking a lot of roundabout questions, but they were working up to something specific.

He waited them out, refusing to let his impatience show. They wouldn't hear anger or frustration when they listened to the interview tape back. They'd hear boredom and compliance.

"So, where were you the night of June first?"

And there it was. They had a time of death—some time the evening of June first. The day *before* the kidnap attempt. Now, they wanted his alibi. Cash blew out a breath. Trying to think of both the truth and how the hell he was going to get out of this. "Monday, right? Izzy's on summer break so our schedule is a little looser than normal, but I spend every night in the same place. In my cabin, on this property, with my daughter."

"Can you take us through that particular night?"

"I don't remember anything specific. But the usual pattern is eating dinner around six. Sometimes here at the main house, but if I remember correctly, we had spaghetti night at the cabin. Then we go play with the dogs until sunset. We go inside, Izzy takes a shower while I clean up the dinner mess. She goes to bed, then I watch TV, or do some reading, and then go to sleep."

"Alone, presumably?"

Cash wanted to scowl. Wanted to yell. Carlyle had been right. They didn't see it as enough of an alibi.

"It's okay. You can tell them."

Cash jerked at the new voice, looked over his shoulder at where Carlyle stood in the entrance to the room. She looked tired, but she was dressed for a morning of dog training. Swiftie sat at her feet, tail softly swishing back and forth.

"Tell them what?" he asked, wholly and utterly confused at what she thought she was doing.

"We've been keeping it on the down-low, but he wasn't alone. We were together."

What the hell was she doing? *Lying* to the cops? He stood and turned to face her, to try to get it through to her whatever she was doing was *not* the way to handle this, without giving anything away to the cops. "Carlyle."

But her gaze was steady on the detectives, her expression stubborn. "It's kind of a secret, but I'd rather tell the truth than have you guys looking in the wrong direction. I was with him. In his cabin. In his bedroom. For most of the night that night."

Chapter Six

"Can anyone corroborate that story?" the detective asked, keeping any thoughts she had on the subject closed behind an easygoing expression.

But Carlyle knew how to lie to cops. She knew how to make them believe it. She *knew*, and she'd made a promise to Izzy. "Like I said, it's a bit of a secret. We've been sneaking around. You know, family can be complicated, and we wanted to see where it went before Izzy got involved. Not to mention my brothers."

Carlyle watched as the two detectives exchanged a look. It wasn't disbelief exactly, but they certainly weren't falling for it hook, line and sinker. The woman wrote down a few lines in her notebook.

Carlyle moved farther into the room. She didn't dare look at Cash's expression. He was probably blowing the whole thing, so she had to focus on the cops. Focus on saving him from his noble self.

"I bet if you asked anyone around here, they'd say the same thing. Maybe they didn't *see* me at Cash's cabin, or know anything was going on, but they've wondered. Noticed little things. Maybe someone will remember something from that night, even."

"So, you're saying you were in Cash Hudson's cabin—"

"*Bedroom*," Carlyle corrected the male cop, hoping to

God her cheeks weren't turning red. She could not actually *think* about being in Cash's bedroom, even as she convinced these cops that was just the usual.

"I saw Carlyle sneak into the main house very early that morning. Coming from the direction of Cash's cabin."

Everyone turned to Mary, who was pushing a little cart with a tray of food on top. She stopped the cart in front of the detectives. "Please, help yourselves. But Carlyle is right. I did see something, and I didn't say anything to anyone about it."

"Why not?"

"My husband is her very protective older brother, and Cash is *my* brother. I thought I'd just keep it to myself until they were ready to be open about it. It wasn't really any of my business what my adult brother and adult sister-in-law were getting up to in the middle of the night."

Carlyle wanted to cheer. Mary was lying. *Mary.* Carlyle might have expected the quick thinking and subterfuge of Anna, but Mary was so proper, so upstanding. But she was also always surprising people.

"What time was this?" the female detective asked, pen poised on the pad of paper.

"I don't know exactly. I'm up and down with morning sickness all night half the time. After midnight, definitely. So morning, but very early. Before the sun was up."

She was so smooth, and not too specific. *Just* specific enough to corroborate Carlyle's story and give a large window of an alibi to Cash. It was a *revelation.*

Carlyle had to look back at the detectives to keep from grinning. She couldn't look at Cash. It would ruin her act, she knew.

"Thank you for your cooperation. We'd like to speak to Anna Hudson-Steele next. She had a run-in with Chessa Scott a while back?"

"She did," Mary said primly. "Help yourselves to food, detectives. My sister will be down once she's done *feeding* her baby." And with that, Mary sailed back into the kitchen.

"What about Hawk Steele? Can he be bothered this morning?" the man asked, with only a *hint* of sarcasm in his tone.

"Yeah, we'll go get him," Cash said. He took Carlyle by the elbow, and she realized she was the *we* in this situation. He pulled her out of the room, down the hallway, and didn't say a word.

When she finally worked up the nerve to look at his expression, it was a cold kind of fury she'd only ever seen on his face that night of the would-be kidnapping.

"If you're going to yell at me, you should probably wait until they're gone," Carlyle muttered under her breath. He didn't drop her arm even though they were out of earshot. He just dragged her along and up the stairs.

"I'm not going to yell at you," he muttered. He knocked softly on Anna and Hawk's door.

Hawk opened it, scowling already. But he was dressed, and Anna was rocking baby Caroline in the corner in her pajamas.

"I take it the cops want to talk to me."

"News travels fast. They asked for Anna first, though."

Hawk's scowl deepened. "I'll handle it."

"Oh, I don't mind talking to them once Caroline's done," Anna said. "Considering how often I have to feed this ravenous barnacle, it's going to be very hard to pin this one on me. They ask you for an alibi?" Anna asked Cash.

"Yeah," Cash said. He kept his expression carefully neutral. "For the night of June first. Carlyle supplied one."

"How did Carlyle supply an alibi for the whole night…"

Anna trailed off. "Oh." Her gaze was sharp—from Cash to Carlyle then back again. "Well."

Carlyle had to fight off another wave of embarrassment as Cash didn't explain it away. He let Hawk and Anna just... believe it was true. And she'd never been one for embarrassment, but this was just...weird.

"I'll go talk to them until you're ready," Hawk said darkly. He bent over and brushed a kiss across Anna's cheek, then Caroline's. "And when you come down, do not be yourself."

Anna grinned up at him. "I could not possibly fathom what you mean, darling."

He grunted, but turned and left the room. He closed the door behind him so Cash, Hawk and Carlyle all stood in the hall.

Hawk paused. "If they get too hung up looking at any of us, whoever actually did it is going to disappear."

Cash nodded grimly, but Carlyle didn't need to nod because hadn't that been her whole point with the fake alibi? This needed to be a concerted effort to not just rely on the cops who had to follow procedures and every viable option.

Hawk strode down the hallway toward the stairs. Carlyle moved to follow, but Cash took her by the arm again and pulled her down the hallway to a room at the end of it. She assumed it was the room he slept in when he stayed at the main house.

He closed the door behind them, and Carlyle tried not to feel nervous. She didn't do nervous. She'd done what was right, what would help. He could be mad at her all he wanted, but she was *right*.

And still, her stomach jittered with worry.

"You were right." He blew out a long breath. "They'll look into Anna because she had a fight with Chessa a long time ago. They'll look into Hawk because Chessa was involved in hurting him, but mostly they think I'm the prime suspect."

"So are you going to thank me for my quick thinking?" she asked, trying for her usual flippant tone.

He glared at her. "I don't like this. Lies come back to bite. Why do you think I let Anna think…" He shook his head. "It's best that only you, me and Mary know the alibi is a lie. I need you to agree to that."

"What about Walker? I don't mind lying to him, but you're going to have to make sure Mary is okay with it."

"Hell, I don't know. I guess that's up to Mary."

"What about Izzy? They're going to want to question her."

"They can go to hell."

"Cash—"

"Don't. Don't start on the she needs to have some choice or power or whatever."

He sounded so…at the end of his rope. Just barely hanging on by a thread. She wanted to soothe him somehow. But now wasn't the time. They had to act. He had to get over this hang-up. "Okay. I won't start on that, but… Izzy has some theories."

"Theories?"

"About how the events might connect. About who the actual target might be. She's smart. She's—"

"Twelve."

"Yeah, Cash. *Twelve.* Not two. She's looking for patterns, links, and she's worried about you. Scared to death *you'll* get hurt in all this. We have to work together. All of us. Maybe the cops will beat us to answers, but maybe they won't. So, let's *all* work together. On the same page. *With* Izzy. If you let her in on this, at least a little, she's not going to be crying in my room worrying that you're going to end up like Chessa."

She hadn't *meant* to let the crying part spill, but she didn't know how to get through his thick skull.

He closed his eyes, clearly in pain—emotional pain. And she couldn't stop herself anymore. She crossed the room to him, put her hand over his heart.

"You're both trying so hard to protect each other that you are shutting each other out, and I don't think that's what either of you want, Cash."

He opened his eyes and looked down at her. A million things swam in the dark depths, mostly bad things. Hurt and worry and she just wanted to *fix* it for him. Her free hand came up and touched his cheek.

"I promise, letting her in isn't going to ruin her life. Giving her some agency isn't going to fling her into danger. She's already *in* danger. Let's give her the tools to find some power. And protect the hell out of her while we do. All of us. Your siblings. Mine. And your amazing daughter. I have faith in the Hudson-Daniels machine, Cash. Do you?"

He inhaled slowly and she knew she should take her hand off his face. She knew she should step away.

But she didn't. As the moment stretched out, she just stood there, while he slowly let out his breath and didn't move away.

But when he inhaled again, he patted her hand, as if she was a child, and then stepped back. "Thanks, Carlyle," he said, though his voice was rough. "You're right. Let's get everyone together and go from there."

Then he left her in that room, heart feeling bruised and wrung out, tears she didn't understand in her eyes. But she'd gotten her point across.

Everyone together.

She had to believe that would matter.

CASH TENDED TO avoid big family meetings. He didn't like Izzy getting too involved in whatever was going on, particularly ever since Izzy had witnessed a gun to Anna's head last year. But Carlyle had been insistent and… He wanted her to be wrong about it, but no matter how he looked at it, he couldn't convince himself she was.

She understood Izzy's position too well. And she was right, the Hudson-Daniels machine was better than any police department in the world.

She just kept being right. He rubbed at his chest, where she'd put her hand. Like she could impress upon him all these truths he'd been avoiding for years. Like she could just crumble all those walls he'd built to keep his daughter safe.

And failed, time and time again.

He could admit failure. You couldn't be a parent for twelve years, particularly under the circumstances in which he'd been a parent, and think you couldn't fail, but gathering up all his siblings to discuss that failure felt a bit *much*.

But they all gathered, in the big living room with his siblings where they'd once crushed together on the couch to watch movies. Their parents would always make a huge batch of popcorn and then curl up on the love seat that he now had at his cabin.

He'd always thought those first few years without them would be the hardest. Being a teenager, not knowing what happened to them. But it was now. With Izzy nearing the age he'd been when he lost them. With his memories of them getting fuzzier and fuzzier.

When he was so tired, so exhausted and wrung out he wanted to lay the weight of all this awfulness on someone else's lap. Just for a minute or two.

He supposed, if he let himself get over the whole *failure* part, this was as close to that as he was going to get. Anna in Hawk's lap on the armchair, Caroline's baby monitor on the little table next to them. Palmer and Louisa and Grant and Dahlia shoved together on the couch, in the almost exact same position—his brother's arm around his fiancée. Walker and Mary on the window seat. Zeke, Walker and Carlyle's brother who lived in Sunrise and kept somewhat more separate from everyone else, stood next to them, arms crossed over his chest.

He almost perfectly mirrored Jack, who stood on the other side of the room, looking grim, while Izzy and Carlyle lay on the floor with the dogs.

Cash never ran these meetings. He'd been as separate as he could be. Now, this was his problem and he had to take charge.

"So, we all know what happened. Chessa was murdered on June first. Sometime at night. The police have now questioned me, Hawk, Anna and Jack. What's next?" Cash looked at Jack. Since he was the sheriff, had even worked for Bent County for the first few years of his police career, he'd have an idea of their investigative tactics.

"Now that they have a time of death, likely, they'll start looking into her movements that night. If they can narrow down the location of the last place she was seen alive, they'll try to find people who saw her, get their impressions."

"Any idea where she was found?"

"They're being really careful because they don't want me to know too much and pass it on to you. But Chloe talked to the coroner. Didn't get much, but she thinks she was found *in* Bent."

"My money is on Rightful Claim. The saloon there? If Chessa was in Bent, she didn't pass up going to a bar." Anna turned to her husband. "We could go have a night on the town. Ask some questions."

Hawk shook his head. "The guy who owns that saloon is married to Detective Delaney-Carson," Hawk said, referring to the female detective. "I don't think going there and questioning anyone is a good idea if it might get back to the detective. We need Bent County to think we're just waiting for them to solve it."

"I could do it," Zeke said. "I know how to be stealthy, and I don't have as known of a connection to you guys. At least in Bent." He turned his gaze from Anna and Hawk to Cash.

Because, apparently, this was somehow *his* deal, when he'd avoided making these kinds of decisions for twelve years.

Cash gave him a nod. "That'll work. Palmer, any fixes for the missing security footage?"

Palmer shook his head. "It's been wiped, that's for sure. I've got a friend over in Wilde seeing if he can't do better than me, but it's not looking good. But to that point, Chessa wasn't acting alone. Clearly. She didn't have that kind of skill or background. By my way of thinking, whoever killed her worked with her on that kidnapping attempt."

"It wasn't Chessa at my window the other night," Izzy said. She'd moved so she was pressed against Carlyle, like she was looking for some comfort. Cash waited to feel some kind of…discomfort or jealousy, but he could only feel gratitude that Izzy had different people to lean on, gain confidence from.

God knew Carlyle had more than her share.

"How do you know that?" Jack asked gently.

"I don't know. It just…wasn't. She…she's like…" Izzy threw her hands in the air, clearly struggling to find the words she wanted to. "She's just not careful. She would have just…like bashed in the window or something. Aunt

Anna, when she came here that one Christmas, you said she was a bull in a china shop. Always had been."

Anna nodded. "Yeah, *careful* isn't Chessa's usual style, but... She knew how much trouble she could get into. Maybe she figured out how to be stealthy."

Izzy shook her head and so did Carlyle.

"Whoever ran into me was pretty...solid," Carlyle said. "From everything you guys have told me, Chessa was shorter, less substantial. Whoever knocked me to the ground was taller than me. Wider. If Chessa was involved, it wasn't her at the window, and it wasn't her doing the security stuff. Maybe we need to consider the fact she wasn't involved at all?"

Cash looked at her. *Knocked me to the ground* when she'd been stabbed. Because there was the whole truth and then there was being careful about not overwhelming Izzy with it. He had to appreciate the fact Carlyle saw some nuance and balance to the situation.

Carlyle dipped her head, whispered something into Izzy's ear. Izzy frowned, but then she nodded. "I don't think the kidnapping thing was about me. Or Chessa, really. I know she told Uncle Hawk she wanted to sell me or whatever, but that was just about getting money."

Cash felt like he'd been stabbed. She'd *heard* that? When he'd worked so hard to keep her in the dark about the worst things Chessa could be.

"Go on. Say the rest," Carlyle encouraged, while Cash reeled. But Izzy wasn't done dropping bombs.

Izzy took a deep breath. "I think someone wants to hurt *you*, Dad. Or maybe the whole family. But mostly you."

And Cash was left utterly speechless.

Chapter Seven

Carlyle watched as the color simply leached out of Cash's face. It made Carlyle feel awful for him, but at the same time, she thought that reaction was good. He wasn't denying it out of hand.

He knew it wasn't just possible, it was a *reasonable* theory. Which meant they could act on it, instead of wasting time trying to convince him it was possible.

It had taken Izzy a lot of courage to say it to a room full of adults, and no one was arguing with her or discounting her. It warmed Carlyle's heart, because her brothers had *always* meant well, but they'd been young men saddled with the responsibility of a little sister. They'd discounted her, scoffed at her, and often made her feel foolish without *meaning* to.

But the Hudsons knew better. They were mature, and had the experiences and enough of a framework to all instinctively give Izzy the feeling she'd helped.

"If someone was targeting Cash, Chessa would be at the top of the list," Jack said, not as a counterpoint, but more thoughtfully. Like thinking Izzy's point through. "Izzy is on to something, but I don't think we can fully discount Chessa's involvement."

"Absolutely. Chessa could very well be involved," Carlyle offered. "But she's not the *point*. She's…"

"A pawn," Anna finished for Carlyle. "She was a pawn last year. Darrin Monroe used her because she hated us. But his goal wasn't her goal. She wasn't…with it enough to have a clear goal. It was about feeding the addiction. Not about like…actual plots and plans."

"She could have gotten mixed up with someone who had the plots and plans, and she was the one who chose the target," Cash said grimly, and with a careful look at his daughter.

Because even though by all accounts Chessa was a bit of a monster, wanting to sell her own child, Cash cared about how that affected his daughter.

"I think we should go back and look through what happened with the guy who wanted revenge on you guys. Who was involved, beyond him and Chessa. Let me look at the file or report or whatever. Yours or Sunrise's. Maybe I'll see something you guys didn't since you know all the players." Carlyle looked around the room. She couldn't make out what everyone's expressions meant, but there was really only one person who mattered.

She glanced at Cash.

But it was Jack who spoke. "He just had a personal vendetta against us. Darrin is in a high-security psychiatric hospital, so I just don't see how it could connect."

"I don't either. Not yet. And maybe it doesn't. But isn't that what we do?" Mary asked. "Pull threads until something unravels. This is another thread to pull, and it's less likely to draw the attention of Bent County. Zeke sees if he can gather anything in Bent. Carlyle goes over that case. Chloe keeps trying to see what other information she can get out of Bent County to pass along to Jack."

The conversation from then on was more logistics than anything else, and Izzy practically climbed into Carlyle's lap. Carlyle held the girl close, hoping Cash didn't see this as a failure. That just because Izzy was upset didn't mean she shouldn't be here. Upset was just part of the deal when your mother was murdered, whether you loved her or not.

When they finally started to scatter, Cash reached down and helped Izzy to her feet. "Come on. Time for bed." Copper got up too, so Carlyle got to her feet. Before Cash led Izzy away, Izzy turned and threw her arms around Carlyle.

She hugged the girl back, reluctant to let go. There was no way to convince Izzy she was safe. Carlyle knew that better than anyone, but she was understanding more and more the lengths her brothers had gone to try. The lengths Cash and his family went to try.

When Izzy finally released her from the hug, she grabbed her hand. "Come with," she said.

Carlyle didn't know where she was coming with to, but she wasn't about to argue with the girl. She let Izzy lead her, side by side with Cash, deeper into the house and up the stairs, Copper and Swiftie following along.

They stopped at a door and Izzy turned to Carlyle and wrapped her arms around her one more time. "Thank you," she whispered, and squeezed tight.

Carlyle hugged her back, running a hand over her braid. "No thanks necessary, Iz. Friends help each other out."

Izzy's mouth curved, the first smile Carlyle had seen on her face all day. Cash opened the door and silently led Izzy inside with Copper. She was sharing Caroline's nursery, because it was in the center of the house, and because there was a video baby monitor in there.

Caroline was already asleep in her crib, so Izzy had to sneak in quietly. Cash moved behind her, tucked her in. They whispered something to each other, and Carlyle knew she shouldn't stand there and *watch*, but she couldn't help herself.

He loved his daughter *so* much. There was no doubt he'd do anything and everything to keep her safe, and the fact he wasn't perfect at it only made the whole thing…that much more poignant. That you could love someone so hard, and fail again and again, and just keep trying.

It put a weird lump in her throat, and a longing in her heart she didn't understand.

When Cash exited the room, pulling the door carefully closed behind him, he gestured for her to follow him. She didn't know what else to do. All worked up internally, she really wanted to go hide in her room and work on some kind of…protection against all this *feeling*.

Instead, she followed him into the bedroom from yesterday.

The bedroom he was staying in.

He closed the door behind them, leaving the dog on the other side.

It was nothing, Carlyle *knew* it was nothing and yet she could also feel the heat climbing into her cheeks. Her stomach fluttered at the mere…thought.

Get it together.

"That was productive," she offered, trying to sound her usual irreverent self…and fearing it came out more like the squeaky words of a coward. "The Hudson-Daniels show is on a roll."

"Between Zeke going to Bent and you going over an old case, it's sounding more like the Daniels show."

"Does it matter who's doing it if it gets done?" she countered, feeling defensive and sympathetic all at the same time.

"No, it doesn't," he said, with a kind of firmness that brooked no argument. Or the kind of firmness someone used when they were trying to convince themselves of something.

He said nothing else, made no effort to break the silence or explain to her why she was here.

"So…" She had no idea why he'd brought her in here, and the longer they stood, in his room, alone, on opposite sides of a messily made *bed*, the more she wanted to jump out of her own skin.

"Look, there needs to be some effort to…" He trailed off, never finishing his sentence.

"To what?" she asked, since she sincerely had no idea what he was talking about.

He opened his mouth, closed it, then a knock interrupted whatever he was going to come up with. He sighed heavily, then gave her a sharp look.

"Look rumpled."

"What?"

"You came up with this alibi. Now you gotta play along with it." Then he stalked over to the door, clearly unhappy with the whole situation. Cash opened the door, and her brother stood at the threshold.

When Walker saw *her*, looking rumpled as ordered, sitting on the edge of the bed, his eyes hardened.

So, she grinned at him. "Heya, Walk."

CASH WISHED IT WAS…literally anyone else. Except maybe Zeke. He did not want to deal with either of Carlyle's brothers over something that wasn't even true.

No matter how she'd blushed when he'd closed the door behind them. Which was not something he could think about. Certainly not his body's response to it. Not now. Not ever.

He wasn't thrilled about this turn of events, but he had

to see it through. And if Walker was standing there looking like he might actually take a piece out of him, it meant Mary hadn't spilled the beans about this all being fake.

Which was something. Not that Cash particularly wanted to play along with this fiction, but he felt like he didn't have a choice. They'd used it with the cops, now it just had to be...

"What the hell are you two doing?" Walker demanded.

Carlyle's eyes got real wide, comically wide. Clearly, she was needling her brother. "Talking, Walker. Whatever else could we be up to?" She walked over and stood next to Cash. Too close, judging by the way Walker's gaze got even harder. Cash wouldn't know because he was keeping his gaze resolutely anywhere but on her.

"Laying it on a little thick, Car," Cash muttered, torn between a dark kind of amusement, because it *was* funny, and just...wishing he was not in the middle of any part of this situation.

Carlyle moved to face him, so he *had* to look at her, and she trailed her finger down his chest—*Jesus*—and smirked. "That's what I do, babe."

Then she flounced out of the room, over Walker's sputtering. Swiftie got up and followed her down the hallway.

Cash regretted every decision that had led him here.

Particularly when Walker's rather large hands clenched into fists. "I want to know what's going on between you and Carlyle. What you think you're doing with my baby sister, who's a good seven years younger than you."

Cash might have felt some sympathy for Walker, what with having two younger sisters of his own. He understood the need to be protective, to maybe warn a guy off. But one of those sisters was Walker's wife, so... "What's the age difference between you and Mary again?"

"Less than seven," Walker said darkly.

"Yeah, by like a *month*," Cash replied with as much sarcasm as he could muster. "You don't have much of a leg to stand on, you know. My sister got kidnapped because of you. I don't recall getting involved." Because he never did, did he? And it hadn't helped him at all. "So far, I've given your sister a job and—"

"Yeah, *and*. The *and* is what I'm ticked about."

Cash scrubbed his hands over his face. "Isn't my current circumstance enough of a disaster without whatever this is?"

"Yeah, and you've got my sister involved in it."

"She got herself involved. I tried to stop her. A million, trillion people could try to stop her. She doesn't *stop*. Don't pretend you don't know that."

"She's got a bad habit of wanting to help a lost cause."

Cash laughed, a little bitterly, because boy was he a damn lost cause. "What do you want me to say, Walker? To do? Because unless it involves mind control, we both know *she* is going to do whatever the hell she wants."

"You just steer clear. She doesn't need to get messed up in this. She shouldn't be at those meetings, or in your room, or getting *stabbed*, Cash." Then he turned around, like he'd given a directive he expected to be followed wholesale, no argument.

Which was right. Cash shouldn't be able to argue with it, because it was all things he'd said about his daughter, and if he didn't have a daughter, things he'd likely be saying about his sisters.

But…maybe Carlyle had gotten to him because he could see this too easily from *her* point of view. Not Walker's or his.

"Maybe you don't give her enough credit, Walker."

Walker stopped at the doorway. Turned, slowly. Cash

was sure it was meant to be intimidating, but he was too tired and Walker wasn't any older or stronger or different than him.

If anything, they were too damn much alike.

"Excuse me?" he asked, very slowly.

"So far, your sister has proven my instincts wrong at just about every turn. You think I was going to let my daughter sit in the middle of that meeting, talking about her mother's murder? Hell no. That was all Carlyle. Because as she likes to keep telling me, she's been in Izzy's shoes."

There was a flicker of something in Walker's expression that Cash recognized all too well. Guilt. Because boy had they walked damn similar paths.

"I get it. Better than anyone, probably. The way you feel. The things you do to protect someone you love who you see as more vulnerable. But Carlyle's not. No more vulnerable than you. Than me. She's smart and she's strong. Not invincible, though she might think it, but the thing she seems most adamant about is that she doesn't need someone to swoop in and save her or hide her away from the bad things. And I realize I'm not a great catch, but I'm hardly a bad thing you need to save her from."

"Maybe. I know she can't see it that way, but for *me*, I have been Carlyle's dad from the time she was Izzy's age, whether any of us liked it or not. So it doesn't matter how old, how not-vulnerable, how whatever she gets, I'm always going to do what I can to protect her. It's what fathers do, and I know you know that."

"Yeah, I do know that. Understand it. But recall, we've got our own orphan situation over here. There's a reason no one bashed your face in when you started up with Mary. Because we could all see you were so head over heels in love with her, you'd destroy yourself before you hurt her on purpose. It isn't always about…protecting them from every difficulty."

"You saying you're in love with my sister?" Walker asked, a little *too* casually.

Damn. "I'm saying, do you really think I'm going to do anything to mess her up? Do you, knowing my family, knowing me, really think she needs you to butt in? Bud, she'll kick my ass from here to Kentucky if she sees fit. And I can't go anywhere, so I'll just have to suck it up and have my ass kicked."

"Maybe if you didn't have the kid, but she's got a soft spot for Izzy. She won't hurt you if it'd hurt your daughter."

Cash wondered if the blows would ever just stop, give him a chance to breathe, adjust, move on and heal one bruise before another came. "Fine, I give you permission to kick my ass if it comes to it. Happy?"

Walker studied him. "I'll send Zeke to do it. He's meaner." But he grinned, a bit too much like Carlyle for comfort. Then he sobered up. "I know you're a good guy, Cash. That's not the issue. The issue is you got a kid to put first, and at some point… Carlyle deserves a life where she gets to come in first."

"I'm sure she does," Cash agreed, surprised to find that it…hurt more than it should that he agreed with Walker. Because this was all pretend. Not real. So it didn't matter what he couldn't give her.

And never would.

Chapter Eight

With extra people in the main house, Carlyle felt even less like she could sleep with the lights on. Which meant sleeping was a bit of a bust, and now that she'd been traumatized and stabbed from something as simple as looking out the window on a starry night, that was hardly the relaxing pastime it had once been.

Maybe she just needed a snack. Something heavy and fatty that would make her nice and sleepy. She left her room, ready to sneak over to the kitchen, but something...creaked above.

Someone was moving around upstairs. And considering there were what felt like a hundred people in this house, it could be anyone. Hell, it could be the house settling.

But her gut had been right last time. Someone bad *had* been outside. Maybe it was unlikely anyone *bad* had gotten upstairs, but it wasn't *impossible*.

She looked at Swiftie. The dog would make too much noise if she followed. Carlyle crouched, looked the dog in the eye. "Stay," she whispered firmly.

Heart pounding, nerves humming, she snuck her way up the stairs, being careful to try and avoid the ones that squeaked. She'd learned long ago to make sure she knew how to move around anywhere she was living without making a noise.

But when she carefully crested the stairs, the hallway was illuminated by a night-light plugged into the wall. There was no lurking shadow or stranger.

Just Cash.

Not walking up and down the hallway, not going from one room to another. Just sitting on the hallway floor, his back to the wall right next to Izzy's door. Carlyle figured she should probably turn around, sneak back downstairs and...leave it. Leave this.

But he looked so *alone*, and she just couldn't stand it. She purposefully made some noise before stepping into his line of vision.

His head snapped up, but once he recognized her, some of the tenseness in his shoulders released. "What are you doing up?" he asked in a whisper when she got close enough.

"Can't sleep." She didn't need to ask him what he was doing. It was pretty obvious. She went ahead and moved into a sitting position on the floor next to him. "Going to sit out here all night?"

"No." He had his legs out in front of him, his head resting back against the wall. Kind of the picture of defeat, but she knew he wasn't defeated. Because he'd never give up while his daughter might be in danger. That was just the kind of guy he was. Why else would she be halfway to messed up over him?

"I know she's okay," he said, like Carlyle had demanded an explanation when she hadn't. "But sometimes..."

"I think you've got all the fairest reasons to be a little paranoid. But you know what I do when I can't sleep?"

He looked over at her, one eyebrow raised. "Roam the house? Sneak around in the dark getting stabbed?"

She kept her laugh quiet. "Yeah, that. And find something

productive to do. Let's go unearth that case file you guys were talking about tonight. We can go over it together until we're too sleepy to fight it."

"I wasn't involved in that case. I don't get involved in cases." He said it so firmly.

She understood this wasn't stubbornness for the sake of being stubborn, but something he needed to believe. That by keeping his nose out of things, he wasn't just protecting Izzy *now*, but always had been. That the choice, the sacrifice had been the *right* one.

But Carlyle knew all too well sometimes there was no *right* choice, there was only what you did to survive. Physically. Emotionally.

Sometimes it felt like she understood him better than she understood herself. Because she understood what he felt, but not why she was being all soft and gooey over this mess of a man in the privacy of her own head.

But here she was. "Involved or not, you were there. And so was Izzy." *And so was Chessa*, but she didn't say that out loud because she didn't think it needed to be said. She got back to her feet, held out a hand. "Come on. Better than sitting here like a sad weirdo."

He snorted, and it took him a second or two, but he finally took her offered hand and let her help him up. She wanted to keep holding onto his hand, but she dropped it. She might be gooey, but she was no fool.

"She wouldn't be happy to find you out here," Carlyle said. Not an admonition, just a reminder.

He shook his head. "I know."

Carlyle nodded, then turned away from him and the urge to put her arms around him and *comfort* him. She headed back downstairs, where they'd be able to talk at a more reasonable level and Carlyle knew there was a room full of files.

And they could focus on *that*, not this feeling inside of her.

Swiftie was waiting at the bottom of the stairs, then followed as they made their way to the office.

"Wait here, I'll get the keys," Cash said.

So she waited by the door to the office. She reminded herself she was just…helping him out. Giving him something to do. Giving herself something to do. It was better than going stir-crazy in that little bedroom, desperately trying *not* to think about him.

And his bed.

She nearly jumped a foot high when he returned, because she'd been too busy trying to push that thought away that she hadn't even been listening. He unlocked the door and pushed it open, moving inside first. He went right for a file cabinet, shuffled through some folders, then pulled one out.

He turned to face her, but the room was so crowded with stuff—filing cabinets and security equipment and an array of computers and printers—there wasn't much space at all.

Just them facing each other in a small, dim room. Even the dog had stayed outside the doorway.

It was too small. They were too close. It was too…

"Let's go out into the living room," he suggested.

Carlyle nodded and followed him out to the spacious living room. She sat down on the couch, but then he sat right next to her.

So much for distance.

He opened the file and spread out the contents on the coffee table as Swiftie settled herself under the table. "Jack double-checked earlier. Darrin is still in the state hospital under maximum guard. Jack should have a list of anyone who's visited him by tomorrow, the next day at the latest. So, we'll look into it, but it just feels like a dead end."

Carlyle picked up a few pieces of paper stapled together. It outlined everything that had happened. "Who wrote this account?"

"Everyone. Anna started it with everything she knew, then we each went over it and added things."

Carlyle read the entire document, then went through it line by line to try to work out any players the Hudsons might have overlooked. Chessa had been arrested before Darrin had made an appearance. She'd worked with him to take Hawk against his will, but Chessa was the one who got caught and arrested.

But then she'd been let go. Her bail posted by one of the Hudson ranch hands. A traitor, basically.

"What about this cop who let Chessa go?" she asked, pointing at the name *Bryan Ferguson*.

"What about him? He just followed procedure. Tripp Anthony, on the order of Darrin Monroe, is the one who paid her bail and got her out because Darrin was paying him too. There was nothing out of the ordinary on the cop's side. Just a mistake."

"But wouldn't he know that Chessa wasn't your average jailbird? Wouldn't he know Jack was involved and give him some warning? It seems like an epic screwup to let her go and two hours pass before Jack finds out."

"Jack chewed him a new one, I'm pretty sure. It was all on the up and up, procedure wise. I don't know that it's some great conspiracy when it had been an honest mistake. Jack trusts his team."

She was about to argue with that, but he held up a hand. "*But* we can see what Jack has to say in the morning. Mary's right, it's all just pulling at threads. We pull at them all, no matter how seemingly pointless or wrong, until we have answers."

Carlyle nodded. But she looked at the name. Honest mistakes happened all the time, but a cop should know better.

Cash yawned. "And I think I've hit the wall of exhaustion that *might* let me get a few hours before chores. We should try to get some sleep."

Carlyle nodded and knew she should just…agree. Not chase the desperate desire to keep him right here. "You know, I could hang out in your room. Emerge in the morning. Really let everyone talk. I could sleep in a chair or on the floor or something. Not suggesting we share a bed or anything."

He paused—midstretch—like she'd done something really shocking. But then he dropped his arms, and expressly did *not* look her in the eye.

"Not a terrible idea, but Izzy might see, and I wouldn't want Izzy to get the wrong idea. I'm not sure how she'd feel. I know she loves you, but she's never seen me with anyone before."

Carlyle knew Cash leaned toward *monk*, but she thought it was more a recent phenomenon. He'd been like seventeen when Izzy was born, probably not even twenty when he'd gotten divorced. Surely in his younger years he'd… "Never?"

Cash shrugged. "Weirdly, the disastrous end of my marriage made me a little leery of trying to start something up with someone and a toddler at home makes it a little hard to take a night off and…have fun."

"I call baloney. You've always had like five built-in babysitters."

"Not *always*. Between Jack's work schedule, and Grant being deployed for a while, Anna and Palmer doing the rodeo, Mary going to college. It's not like now. Everyone scattered."

Except him. He'd always been right here. Because of Izzy. "So you just..." She shook her head. She just couldn't believe it. She'd found time to have a little *fun* when she'd been the target of a murderer, so... She narrowed her eyes at him. "You just didn't want anyone to *know* you were off to get laid."

He made a choking noise, which of course was why she'd put it like that.

"Regardless of *why*, I wasn't. I..." He shook his head. "Why are we having this discussion?"

"You're not saying... Like, *all* this what? Decade? Since you've been divorced you haven't once—"

"Please don't say *get laid* again. Carlyle, this is not..." But he clearly couldn't find the words. She didn't know if it was embarrassment or what. She did know she should let it go.

But she couldn't.

"That's a long, long time not to...have *fun*."

"Good night, Carlyle," he said firmly, and stalked off. She heard the stairs squeak under his weight, could track his progress to his room down the hallway.

She sighed. *Ten years.* All because he had a kid at home? No, it had to be more complicated than that. It had to be something about his marriage, about Chessa.

Who was dead. Murdered. And the real thing she needed to focus on. She stayed in the living room, forced herself to go over the report, and not consider any *fun* she could have with Cash Hudson.

CASH WOKE UP in a foul mood. He could blame it on murder and being a suspect and not being able to sleep in his own damn house, but mostly it was the fact that Carlyle asking him about *fun* had really messed with his mind.

Because it was far too easy to imagine having fun with *her*, and considering his ex-wife was dead and he was suspect number one, that was really not the place his mind should be drifting.

Ever. But especially now.

He had long ago convinced himself that sex was unnecessary. That the enjoyment of it—just like booze and carelessness—was for the young and unencumbered. While Palmer had been sleeping his way through half of Sunrise, Cash had considered himself *better*. Or tried to.

Now…

He threw the covers off, trying not to groan out loud. It was early yet, but an early breakfast, a gallon of coffee and some work with the dogs could maybe take his mind off all the annoying caveats it seemed bound and determined to wander down.

Once downstairs, the smell of breakfast filled the air like it usually did. Mary had already been up and about, whipping up her normal spread. They'd really be in for it once she had the baby and had to take some time off from being the organizer and cook and keeping them all in line.

Mary wasn't in the kitchen, but he helped himself to the food out on warmers. When Cash got to the dining room, there was no one to be found except Jack. He was dressed in his sheriff uniform—khaki pants and a perfectly pressed Sunrise polo. He had his phone in one hand and a fork in the other.

"Morning," Cash offered.

"Morning," Jack replied, setting down his phone. "Sleep okay?"

Cash chuckled, only a little bitterly. "Sure. Nothing like a little possible murder charge to really help a guy sleep."

Jack's return smile was wry.

"Carlyle and I went over the file last night. Couldn't sleep. She wants us to look deeper into Deputy Ferguson."

Jack's expression darkened. "I haven't let him forget what a colossal mistake that was. But the kid is ineffectual at best. Not a cold-blooded killer."

"I know. But what have we got to lose to let her poke into him? Maybe it unties some other knot."

Jack nodded. Not because he thought he was wrong about Ferguson, but because this was how you investigated. And maybe their expertise was cold cases, but it was the same. The way he saw it, they were trying to avoid a cold case.

Just as much as they were trying to avoid him going to jail.

And as much as he should focus on Ferguson, avoiding jail, etcetera, all he could think about was Carlyle. What she'd said last night, and why she'd made him question if he'd been doing the right thing all these years by avoiding *fun.*

In front of him sat his role model, so to speak. "You've been single forever."

Jack paused with the fork full of egg halfway up to his mouth, then set it down on the plate. "I'm sorry. What?"

"If you have a night out on the town, you certainly keep it on the down-low. I've never once met a woman you were dating. At least, not since *you* were in high school, which I'll be kind and point out was a very long time ago."

Jack blinked. Once. His face had gotten very carefully blank. "I'll repeat myself. *What?*"

"I'm just trying to work out why you've kept yourself

living like a monk all these years. I know why *I* do. It made sense for a while, but it doesn't anymore."

Jack's voice took on that holier-than-thou, I'm-in-charge iciness. "I don't see what business it is of yours, Cash. I don't see why we're having this conversation."

"I spent ten years quite convinced I was making the best, most right choice for Izzy by staying away from even a hint of…fun. I assumed you were making the same choice for us. But here we are, all adults. Most of your little chicks married. Why still live like a monk?"

"If this is because you decided to hook up with Carlyle and think I need some kind of…encouragement to go have *fun*, I feel like I should remind you of something far more important. You are the main suspect in the murder investigation of your ex-wife and your daughter's mother. Don't concern yourself with my personal life."

"Or lack thereof?"

"Sure. Right. Just… Can we focus on Ferguson?"

Cash had the totally foundation-crumbling realization that his brother was lying. He *did* have a personal life, or thought he did. Hidden somewhere.

But now was not the time to dig into it.

Probably.

He heard someone in the kitchen, and since Swiftie pranced in and took a seat under the table, Cash figured it was Carlyle.

Then Carlyle appeared, plate piled high. "Morning, boys," she said, sliding into the seat next to Cash. She gave the first bite of food to Swiftie, which Cash should scold her for.

But he didn't.

"Sounded a bit tense. Are we bickering in here?" She made a little tsk-tsking sound.

And Cash had the fully out-of-body, out-of-character impulse to follow Carlyle's example. Irreverent. Never afraid to say the wrong thing, the shocking thing.

"I was just talking to Jack about relationships."

"Juicy."

"I'm beginning to think he has a secret one."

Carlyle's eyes widened. Jack's glare was *glacial*. Cash couldn't help but grin.

"You've really rubbed off on him, Carlyle," Jack said, standing. "Enjoy each other's company while it lasts, I suppose. Because if we don't figure out the *true* concerns of the day, Cash might be spending his mornings talking with the other inmates in Bent County Jail."

And with that, he left.

Carlyle let out a low whistle. "I've never seen him react that way, even to Anna. Why are you picking on your poor brother?"

"Misery loves company?"

She laughed. "What did he say about Bryan Ferguson?"

"He stuck with his initial assessment but gave you free rein to poke into him as you see fit. If you find a lead, he'll follow it." She shoveled some eggs into her mouth and nodded along.

"Excellent," she said.

And he found he couldn't quite stop looking at her. She wasn't fear*less*, but she did a hell of a job acting it. She wasn't reckless with things that were important, but she clearly only counted *people* as important, and his daughter was one of those people. She had a whole different outlook on the world, but at its core the things she valued were the same as the things he valued.

A strange, twisting and oddly weight-lifting realization to have.

She must have noticed his staring. She turned to him,

those expressive blue-gray eyes confused as she wiped at her face. "What? Egg on my face?"

"No. Nothing," he replied, because he didn't have the words for *what*, but he was starting to think he needed to figure them out.

Chapter Nine

Carlyle used her beat-up old laptop to do a rudimentary search on Bryan Ferguson. While she was at it, she started looking into the ranch hand who'd facilitated the payment of the bail. He'd died, but that didn't mean there weren't connections somewhere.

Her entire life had been about following the strange, twisting turns of connection. And then avoiding them when she could.

When she thought her eyes would cross, she went outside and over to the dog barn. It was technically her day off, but she would needle Cash into giving her some work to do. She had to work out her body so her mind—which was going in circles—didn't drive her over the edge.

She'd have liked to have been the one teaching Izzy how to shoot, but in the end that job had gone to Grant, who had the most patience out of anyone. Besides, with the stitches, no one wanted her repeatedly shooting a weapon, no matter how well she could handle it.

So, she went to the dog barn instead. Cash had all kinds of dogs. So there was always all kinds of work to do. She tended to avoid the paperwork if she could. She much preferred the training and being outside.

Swiftie followed her over to where Cash had three of

his younger dogs. He had Izzy up on a horse, and Carlyle quickly realized this was less about training the dogs themselves, and more about giving Izzy the opportunity to train.

He stood, elbows resting on the top of the fence while Izzy took the horse through a walk then a gallop, and shouted different commands to the dogs. Carlyle came to stand beside Cash.

"It's your day off," he said by way of greeting.

"I knew you were going to throw that in my face. I needed a break from my computer. Consider today volunteer work."

He rolled his eyes, but they both stood and watched as Izzy expertly put the dogs and horse through their paces. Carlyle grinned. "Damn, she's a natural, isn't she?"

"It comes with growing up on a ranch surrounded by animals, but she's got a special touch with them, that's for sure." All proud dad. She wanted to lean her head against his shoulder and just enjoy the moment.

If she said that to anyone, they'd think it out of character. She was loud. She was wild. Not traditional, not *soft*.

But sometimes, that armor she'd spent so long building started to feel heavy, like it needed to be taken off.

She sighed and watched Izzy maneuver the horse and command the dogs, all the while keeping a respectable space between her and Cash. Little glimpses of the woman Izzy would grow up to be someday flashed through her mind.

Carlyle watched, but no matter how much she wanted a distraction, her mind kept going back to the problem at hand. Izzy as a kid. Izzy as a woman. It got her thinking. Did she need to look back *further* into the cop's and the former ranch hand's lives? Not just rap sheets—Tripp a small, petty one up to his involvement last year, Ferguson nothing—but maybe earlier in their lives to try and find a connection to each other.

Izzy gave a sharp command to the dogs, and two of the three immediately obeyed. Carlyle tapped her fingers on the fence, watching, thinking.

Cash put his hand over her tapping fingers, stilling them. "Worrying?"

"Thinking," she replied.

He did *not* withdraw his hand, and she held herself very still, trying not to react. Trying not to think anything of it. Friendly gesture. Simple gesture. Clearly just annoyed with her tapping.

"I feel like that should be concerning to me."

She grinned at him. "Me thinking *is* very concerning. This Ferguson guy. What are the chances I can sweet-talk him into saying something he shouldn't?"

Cash's expression was very…odd. She kind of expected him to laugh or lecture her about not getting too involved. But this was neither of those things, and she didn't know what to do with it.

"Probably not the right tactic. Ferguson says to anyone you were…whatever, that's going to poke a hole in that alibi you just had to give me. *We're* supposed to be secretly engaging in sleepovers, remember?"

She glanced over at him, meeting that dark gaze. And there *was* something different in it. Or her brain was a little fuzzy because his very *large*, calloused hand was still resting over hers. "Yeah, I remember," she said.

Breathlessly. Like some kind of *fool*.

"If you've got some questions for Ferguson, let's bring them to Jack. See if he can ask them."

"Is Jack talking to you right now?"

Cash laughed, the corners of his eyes crinkling. He adjusted his cowboy hat, finally took his hand back. "Ah, he's just a bit prickly in the mornings."

"And every other time I've interacted with him. Well, unless Izzy is around. He does have a soft spot for her." Carlyle kept her gaze on the little girl, the whole thing... overwhelming for reasons she couldn't quite articulate.

She just knew that she'd been hard on Cash when it came to how he treated Izzy. She'd been telling him what he'd done wrong. So maybe he deserved to know what he'd done right too. "For anything you think you didn't give her, family matters. My brothers were everything, even when I was trying to get them to give me some space. They were my foundation. She doesn't just have you, she has all of them, and all of this."

"Kinda luck of the draw."

"Maybe. But you could have moved somewhere else. Gotten farther away from cold cases and danger. They don't need you to run the ranch and you don't need them to run your dog business. You stayed for yourself, but you stayed for her too."

"And how are you so sure about that?"

When she looked over at him, her heart hammered against her chest. His expression was...different. Not that *woe is me* or determined, protective dad mode. Something more open. Something more...

She didn't know. So she put her armor back in place, flashed that grin. "I am a keen observer of human nature." But she couldn't keep up the act. "You're not so hard to figure out."

"You are," he replied, so seriously.

She scoffed, or tried to, but her throat was a little tight. "I don't see how."

"You're an excellent mask wearer. I should know. But, per usual, Izzy gets under it. No one can resist Izzy."

"She's the best."

"Yeah. And there's a softy under all the *Carlyle* of it all."

Carlyle gave a fake injured sniff. "I do not know what you're referring to."

He laughed. *Again.* He was smiling. *At her.* And there was something warm and wonderful and *awful* blooming in her chest. She should look away, walk away, lock herself up with the computer and find him some answers.

But her phone rang, and she jumped at the loud, surprising jangle. Less than steady, she pulled her phone out of her pocket. She had to clear her throat to talk.

"It's Zeke. I'll, uh, be right back." She swiped her finger across the screen, turned her back on Cash and took a few steps away. "What?" she demanded.

"Hi to you too."

"I'm working."

"Today's your day off."

"Yeah, but I'm working on case stuff."

"Yeah, me too. I was just calling to see if you'd come up with anything I should be on the lookout for tonight in Bent. Any people I should ask around about being seen with Chessa, that kind of thing."

Not a bad idea. "Bryan Ferguson and Tripp Anthony. Don't necessarily bring up Chessa connecting to them. Just see if you get any kind of reaction from it, some idea of if anyone knew them or what they think about them."

"And if I do get some information?"

"Just file it away. Come out to the ranch for breakfast tomorrow and we'll go over what you find."

"You getting too deep in this, Car?"

"Probably. Why?"

Zeke sighed. "You should be out having some fun or

something. Not getting dragged into more investigations and danger and running. Haven't you had enough of that?"

"Maybe I *like* danger. I'd think *you'd* understand that, mister spy operative."

"Former. I'm enjoying the quiet life."

"My butt," she muttered, turning to look back at Cash and Izzy. Izzy had gotten off the horse and she and Cash were standing next to it, watching the dogs run and tumble over each other.

In the middle of all this, they were laughing.

Carlyle didn't care what kind of fool it made her, she wanted to be part of it.

CASH KNEW SHE'D walked away to talk to her brother in private because they were discussing the murder case and what *they* were doing about it. Which made him uneasy, because he didn't like the idea of them planning something on their own.

And it had nothing to do with her suggesting sweet-talking anybody. Or mostly not about that.

Izzy was chattering on about music and concerts and her usual twelve-year-old stuff and it made him want to believe everything was going to be okay. If she could be worried about cute drummers and the importance of musical *eras*, then maybe he could…do that too.

Maybe not worry about cute drummers but allow himself the bandwidth to focus on more than danger and protection. He wasn't sure he knew how to do that anymore. It had become such a habit, such a comfort zone. Shrank his world down until it was just him, Izzy and dogs.

But it hadn't saved her from trauma, from danger. Maybe he needed to…open up again. Maybe the real lesson in all of this was that he couldn't control the world or the people around him, but he could control the hours and minutes here, and how he thought about them.

He went through the rest of the day making a conscious effort to do just that. To engage in frivolous conversations with Izzy, even when he was walking her to and from the stables to the house in a nod toward keeping her safe. To take a fussy Caroline from a very frustrated and frazzled Anna.

"She's a demon bent on world destruction," Anna said darkly, collapsing onto the couch.

"Like mother, like daughter," Cash replied, making Anna laugh. He walked Caroline in the same relentless circle he used to walk Izzy in when it was the only thing that would put her to sleep. Once Caroline was asleep, and so was Anna, Cash put Caroline in her crib in her room, put the baby monitor speaker next to a sleeping Anna, then checked in on Mary and Izzy. They had their heads together, cooking up something for dinner. He did his routine chores, and he didn't let the darkness of Chessa's murder invalidate all the light in his life.

Carlyle had been right. He could have left. He could have secreted Izzy away any of the times danger came knocking at their door. And he had, in a way, by keeping her cooped up in that cabin. But he'd never been able to dream of raising her without his family, without the legacy of this ranch. Even when trauma and tragedy followed, this was home.

So when the house was dark and quiet, and Izzy was tucked safely into bed, he went down to Carlyle's room.

Because she was a different kind of light he'd *never* allowed himself to have, and maybe it was time to change that.

When she opened her door, she didn't *startle* exactly, but she definitely hadn't been expecting him. Maybe she hadn't really been expecting anyone.

"Hey. What's up?" Swiftie's tail thumped over in the corner. Cash gave her a little hand signal that had the dog trotting out of the room.

"Nothing in particular. Just thought I'd see if you'd found anything new about Ferguson or Tripp." Starting with murder cases. Lame, even for someone as rusty as him.

She was frowning at Swiftie's retreating tail, but then shook her head and turned and walked toward her bed, where a laptop and a notebook and papers were strewn about. She gestured toward them with some frustration. "Not really. There has to be a connection between these two. Why these two guys, you know? How did that Darrin guy get them to help him? But I'm coming up damn empty and it's irritating the hell out of me."

He should use that as a segue to discuss other things, but he couldn't seem to make himself. "Ferguson wasn't a target. He just happened to be the one handling bonds that night."

Carlyle shook her head. "I don't buy that. If it had been Jack or Chloe, would Darrin have sent Tripp to pay her bail? Hell no. It was more careful, more targeted. Too many people would have had to know Tripp was a ranch hand here."

"So they waited till the least likely person was handling it."

"Maybe." Probably, in fact. He didn't want to tell her that if there was a connection, surely someone would have found it by now, when it seemed so important to her to find one. So, he changed the subject.

"Any word from Zeke?"

"No. I told him to come over in the morning and give us an account of what he found, if anything. He'll probably hang out at the bar until at least around it closes. I don't think a lot of baddies are out at—" she glanced over at the clock on her nightstand "—ten fifteen."

"You never know."

She shrugged, and a silence stretched out. This wasn't that unusual. They worked together. Sometimes they dealt in silences. But this one wasn't easy, companionable, or all that comfortable.

So stop beating around the bush, dumbass. "Remember when we were talking about me not…having any fun?"

"Uh, yeah. Sure." She seemed…really uncertain with his change of topic, and maybe that shouldn't amuse him, but managing to set Carlyle a little off-balance—when that was usually her expertise—was kind of nice. "Gonna start hitting the bar scene?"

An attempt to put him off-balance, but not a good one. He only smiled. "No. I don't think so."

"Ah, so…" She cleared her throat, looked at the computer, then at him. No, not at him. Some spot on the wall behind him. "What about it?"

"I thought about it. All day. How I'd pretty much put *fun* out of my head the past twelve years, best I could. But then I got to thinking… In six years, Izzy is going to want to go off to college, I have no doubt, and I'll have to let her. I'll have to let her just…walk away." Which he just…couldn't think about right now. He still had six years. No use mourning something that wasn't here *yet*, even if he had to accept it would be here *someday*.

"Right. So, what, you're going to wait six more years to…have fun?"

He shook his head. "No, you were right. She's not going to thank me for making my entire life her protection. She's going to sit at this dinner table someday, like I did this morning with Jack, and wonder what the hell he's been doing with his life."

"You know, I do have a theory about what Jack's been doing. Or who."

Cash closed his eyes, shook his head. "I don't want to talk about Jack and theories."

"I'm just saying, I went to…"

She trailed off as he stepped closer. Close enough to see the way her dark hair had little glints of red. The way her eyes were too gray to be blue and too blue to be gray. The way her breath kind of caught and then she let it slowly out, watching him not warily, exactly.

Because she was fierce and strong and confident, but she wasn't made of impenetrable armor. He affected her in *some* way, and that was enough to reach out, touch her cheek.

"I like you, Carlyle. You've untied something inside of me that was tied so tight I didn't even know it was there. It was just a weight, holding me down. And you lifted it."

She made an odd kind of sound he didn't know how to characterize, except maybe as a little surprised. Her eyes went bright, and she cleared her throat.

"Just to be clear," she said, and he saw the effort it took her to sound a little cavalier. To not outwardly react to his hand on her cheek. "I had plenty of…*fun* before coming here."

"Hell, Carlyle." She really did have a way. He didn't know why it amused the hell out of him when it really shouldn't have.

"But it wasn't the kind that ever meant anything. Not serious. Not thinking I'd ever be in one place, put down roots, stick. So, I don't exactly know how to do that part."

"Yeah, I've kind of avoided it like the plague after one disastrous marriage."

"Well, look at us, two dysfunctional peas in a pod."

He put his other hand on her other cheek, cupping her face gently, drawing her just a hair closer. It had been so long since he'd felt this—allowed himself to feel it. The heavy thud of his heart, the warmth in his blood. A want he'd closed off a long time ago.

"You know, maybe we should give ourselves a break. Is it dysfunction if we've built fairly good, functioning lives with jobs and family relationships and a lack of jail time?"

Carlyle shrugged, but her mouth curved. "Define *jail time*."

He shook his head, because it didn't matter *why* the things she said amused him, it only mattered that they did. That she lifted those weights away. That something here, between them, worked—no matter how little that made sense.

He lowered his mouth to hers. He paused, just a whisper from contact. Waited until her eyes lifted from his mouth to his gaze. Maybe that's what had first snuck under all his very impenetrable defenses. The unique color, the way—if he looked hard enough—that was the one place he could see that hint of vulnerability.

Then he kissed her, watching the way her eyes fluttered closed, feeling the way she softened into him like melted wax. Like she fit right here, in his arms.

That weight he'd been carrying so long lifted just enough to see the possibility of lifting more. Surviving the weights he couldn't lift. Expanding beyond the tight, hammered-down knot he'd pulled himself into for some bid at control and protection.

But life was in the opening up, not the closing down. So he opened up.

And Carlyle did too.

Chapter Ten

Carlyle woke up to the very odd sensation of her bed moving without *her* moving. And the realization she was very much *not* dressed.

But the *man* getting out of *her* bed was…or in the process of anyway. He reached for a sweatshirt, and she watched the play of muscles across his back. She couldn't imagine when he had time to work out, but as she'd had her hands all *over* those muscles last night, she knew they weren't just for show.

She allowed herself a little dreamy smile because he *was* dreamy. And last night had been…special. Which made a little wriggle of anxiety move through her. Since when did she get special?

He pulled on the sweatshirt and got up. When he looked over his shoulder and met her gaze, he smiled. He bent over the bed.

"You've got time to sleep yet. I've got chores." He brushed a kiss across her forehead, like that was the most natural thing in the world. Like he hadn't been dad-celibate for something like *twelve* years and knew what to do with…this.

She definitely did not know. Because he'd said all that about liking her and thinking she'd lifted some weight and what the hell was a woman supposed to do with *that*?

Particularly if he just…left. Like that was that. Off to do chores.

Was that that? Was this just some kind of…*fun*? Then what was she supposed to do with the whole *I like you* thing, and his daughter, and him? And her whole rooted life that had clearly been a really bad decision?

She could not stand the thought of going through the day not knowing what kind of punch this was so she could roll with it. "This is like…a thing, right?" she asked, before he opened the door to leave. "Not like a…random fun night to blow off a little steam? Because I can do either, but—"

He turned, then cocked his head and studied her from where he stood by the door. When he spoke, it was like he was choosing his words very carefully and she tried to brace herself for the disappointment.

"I don't have a life that allows for blowing off steam, Car."

"You could," she managed to say, though not quite as flippantly and *I-don't-care-what-you-do* as she might have liked. "If you needed to."

He didn't even hesitate. "I don't."

"Okay."

"Do *you* need to?"

She blinked. When she'd said all that stuff about roots? When he kissed her like the entire world had stopped existing? "No, I don't need to."

He smiled. "Good. I'll see you at breakfast."

She couldn't quite manage a smile back, even as he left. She felt a little too…raw and…and…*uncomfortable*.

She sat up in bed, ran her fingers through her tousled hair. *Sex*-tousled hair. Because she had had *sex* with Cash last night.

Multiple times.

Not just blowing off steam. Not *fun*. A physical reaction to the past year. Being friends and attracted to each other was probably always going to lead here. She'd have preferred less *murder* involved, but her life pretty much had always revolved around murder. Why should this be different?

And she was okay with that. She wouldn't be here if she wasn't, but there was something about going from what happened in *just* this room, and *just* between them, to out into the larger Hudson world.

Part of her wanted to crawl under the covers and just hide, and she didn't know why. Because she had never been afraid of anything—or at least hadn't *let* herself dwell in fear. She *acted*.

But this was… It wasn't about danger or fear or any of those things you could *fight*, it was just…her heart. It was easy, in a way, to brazen her way through life when it was all danger and protection and *threats*. Quite the opposite to Cash, she hadn't gone internal, shrunk her world with all the danger. She'd expanded it. Her whole life. It was the only way to survive in her circumstances, to fight out, to ignore fear, to be loud and present and *demanding*.

But both were extremes, and now it seemed they both had to find some middle ground. Maybe that made them good for each other. Maybe that made this all…positive.

But she still didn't know how to deal with his siblings, or hers, or—dear God—Izzy, knowing Cash Hudson had been *inside* her.

She allowed herself a groan then flung herself out of bed. Some old habits still helped a woman get through the day. Flinging her way into the thick of it was the only way she knew how to do this.

She got dressed, brushed out her *very* tousled hair. "You're not a coward. You've never been a coward," she lectured her-

self. Out loud. Then she opened the door, shook her hair
back, squared her shoulders, ready to face whoever and—

Nearly jumped a foot.

Izzy was standing there. Swiftie and Copper on either
side of her, like two little dog sentries.

"Jeez." Carlyle slammed a hand to her heart.

Izzy blinked. "I was just coming to get you for breakfast."

"Oh. Yeah, I'm coming." Carlyle tried to smile as she
stepped out into the hallway, but she knew it stretched all
wrong across her face. She was…uncomfortable. Because
at the end of the day, everything that happened with Cash—
and all his talk about living for himself—didn't matter if
Izzy didn't like the idea.

Izzy came first, and she should. She'd spent her entire
life with her dad apparently never even looking twice at a
woman, and then Carlyle had come along and…

This was why people avoided roots. *This* was why Zeke
had said no way to getting even deeper in the Hudson machine. It wasn't the kind of complicated someone could
just shoot their way out of. She had to deal with untying all
these awful, heavy knots weighted in her stomach.

"Is something wrong?" Izzy asked as they walked toward the dining room.

"No, of course not," Carlyle replied.

But Izzy stopped, blocking Carlyle's forward movement
out of the hallway.

"You'd tell me, right?" she asked, eyebrows furrowed
together as she frowned. A little suspiciously.

Which made Carlyle feel terrible. She bent over a little
so she was eye level with Izzy, put her hand on the girl's
shoulder.

"I promise. Nothing is *wrong.* I'm having a weird personal mental argument with myself about weird personal things. I promise."

Izzy smiled a little, but she studied Carlyle's face. "Is it because you like my dad?"

Carlyle had been calm in the face of so many crises, but none of that had prepared her for *this*. Her eyes widened, her mouth dropped open, and no slick words to talk herself out of this came out.

"So, that's a yes," Izzy said, a bit like… Carlyle was dim.

Carlyle found herself completely speechless.

"He doesn't really do that," Izzy said gently, patting Carlyle's shoulder. "But don't worry. You can be *my* friend. You don't need to be his."

"Uh…" This was…so much worse than she'd imagined. Because Carlyle had the distinct feeling she was…being warned off. When it was a bit too late for that.

"Come on. I'm starving." Then Izzy took her hand and practically dragged her into the dining room.

A lot of the Hudsons were already there. And Zeke was clearly just arriving. Carlyle tried to feel normal instead of like some kind of robot who had to learn to act like humans. Izzy was talking about how she'd helped make the muffins that were on the buffet laid out with food as they went down the line with their plates. Carlyle tried to engage, but she just kept looking at every new person who entered, both hoping it would be and hoping it wouldn't be Cash.

She was going to have to tell him about Izzy's reaction. She was going to have to…do something. But when he entered the room and smiled at her, she knew she shouldn't smile back. She should be…something. Aloof or…cool. But she smiled back because he was just so damn handsome and amazing and…

Really, what did she think she was doing?

He came right over, grabbed a plate, then greeted Izzy before putting some food on his plate. When they moved to sit down, she was standing right next to him, feeling like her heart was going to burst out of her chest. Because Izzy was *right there*, but so were very *visual* memories of last night, and the sweet thing he'd said about her lifting weights and…

Cash ran his hand down her spine before they sat. Casual, but not *friendly*. That was an intimacy, a little bit *more*. Carlyle didn't want to look at anyone, see if they caught that, but she couldn't quite stop herself from glancing at Izzy. Who was frowning at her.

Well, damn.

But she had to focus on Zeke. On the task at hand. Murder and framing and connections.

Not a little girl warning her off her dad.

"The bar was pretty busy. I made the rounds, dropped some crumbs. Lots of people remembered Chessa, but nothing specific about the night she was murdered. At Car's request, I mentioned the cop and the ranch hand. Nothing too obvious," Zeke said once everyone was settled at the table. "No one came out and said anything too direct, but I got the distinct impression that Bryan Ferguson and Tripp Anthony had, on occasion, before last year, not just been seen at Rightful Claim, but had been seen *together* there. And routinely."

"I knew there had to be a connection," Carlyle said, pointing her fork at Cash. Then, because she couldn't help herself even when she was a tangle of Izzy-nerves, at Jack.

"I'm not sure that proves anything," Jack said, but his expression was dark. Angry, clearly. "But we'll look deeper into it. It's a thread to pull." He was clearly mad that he hadn't been right about his employee. But then again, the whole family had been wrong about Tripp, so why should this be different?

Before anyone could say anything else, the doorbell echoed through the house. Everyone paused, but it was Mary as usual who got up to get it.

"Sit," Walker grumbled, standing up himself.

Mary raised an eyebrow at him. "Pardon me?"

He scowled. "With what's going on, you're not answering the door."

Mary's expression didn't change, but she remained very still. "I see."

"You're a brave man, Walker," Hawk muttered from his end of the table, where he held Caroline in one arm and ate with the other hand.

"With danger all around, I don't think it's wise for the—"

"Bud, you better watch every next word," Carlyle said under her breath. Honestly, the fact her brother could still be such a caveman sometimes was ridiculous.

But Mary didn't get all mad or bent out of shape. She didn't glare daggers at her husband—like Anna was currently doing.

The doorbell rang again.

"Go right ahead, Walker. Be a big strong man and answer the door." Mary settled her hands over her bump and gave her husband a bland smile.

Walker swore, clearly realizing he'd dug himself a hole he was going to have to grovel out of later. But whoever was at the door wouldn't wait, so he stalked out of the room.

"I would have punched him," Anna said.

"Some methods are more effective than punching," Mary replied, all pleasant and cool. She was going to rip him a new one.

Carlyle couldn't ignore the fact she wouldn't mind seeing it. She loved the way Mary handled Walker—and most people. Carlyle wished she could emulate it, but she was too much of a Daniels. Bull in a china shop.

Mary would know what to say to Izzy. Mary would know how to handle Cash. Carlyle had a bad feeling she was going to break a hell of a lot of china on this new road she found herself on.

Walker returned, leading the female detective from Bent County into the dining room. Whatever amusement there'd been was sucked out of the room. Everyone went immediately silent and wary. This just...couldn't be good.

The detective's smile was pleasant, but her eyes were sharp. "Good morning," she offered cheerfully. "Sorry to interrupt your meal, but this was a first-thing-in-the-morning kind of deal. And I didn't catch you at your place soon enough." She looked at Zeke. "So, let's talk about what you were doing in Bent last night." Then she helped herself to a seat.

CASH CONSIDERED MAKING an excuse to take Izzy out of the room. He was already on edge about having her listen to what Zeke had found out, but add the detective and it was too much. What twelve-year-old girl would be or should be involved in discussions about her mother's murder? No matter how not part of her life that mother had been.

Cash looked down at her, sitting next to him. She didn't look upset. She didn't seem overwrought. If anything, her expression reminded him a bit of Mary. Cool. Completely collected. Maybe even a little curious. He opened his mouth to say something, to tell her to leave, but hesitated before he could find some gentle way of doing it.

But she turned then looked up at him, all cool and *adult*, and shook her head. As if she knew what he was going to say. She was smart and had been his kid for all these twelve years, so she probably did know.

She didn't want to leave. She wanted to see this through. He didn't like it, but maybe he didn't have to. Maybe sometimes parents had to let their kids see something through, even if it hurt.

"Can I offer you something to eat?" Mary asked the detective.

The detective waved Mary's polite—if a little chilly—offer away. "No, thank you. And I don't want to interrupt your breakfast. I only want some answers as to why you were snooping around Rightful Claim last night, Mr. Daniels. And since you weren't at your apartment this morning, I had the sneaking suspicion you might be here."

"My family is here," Zeke replied.

The detective's smile didn't slip in the slightest. "But they weren't in Bent last night. You were."

"I was just enjoying a drink. I didn't realize your husband was on the Bent County PD payroll." Zeke's return smile was *not* polite. It was sharp and it was mean. Cash didn't know that it was the right tact to take, but God knew he wasn't in charge of Zeke.

The detective remained wholly unfazed by Zeke's demeanor. She'd likely dealt with worse. "My husband tends to notice when people are running a line of questioning in his bar. He *is* married to a detective. He also notices when someone goes poking around in the alley behind the bar. Particularly when it's been the site of a recent investigation."

Zeke had not shared that information with the class. Cash frowned at him.

But Zeke shrugged. "Detective, I talked to some people. I don't know what more you want to hear."

Her eyes flicked briefly to Izzy. Then to Cash. She smiled,

and it seemed genuinely kind. "Maybe we should discuss this more privately," she said to Zeke, but it was easy to see that *private* just meant away from Izzy.

"You don't have to," Izzy said firmly, sounding like an adult. But she took Cash's hand under the table, held on hard. "I know my mother was murdered, and I know you're trying to figure out who did it. I want to be here."

Detective Delaney-Carson studied Izzy's face, then smiled. "Okay. You're free to go whenever you need to though. You get to decide."

Cash wanted to hang on to his frustration and distrust of the woman who clearly had him on her list of suspects, but it was hard to do when she was thinking about Izzy at all, let alone giving her an out.

"Listen," she said, clearly to all of them. "I understand that you all have an investigative business. That you—" she pointed to Anna "—even have an independent private investigator license. I understand and, in fact, am not even opposed to the group of you investigating in whatever ways you can. Legally, and in a way that can actually be used in a court of law, and in a way that does *not* end in some sort of misguided attempt at vigilante justice. But you have to work *with* us."

"Are you going to work with *us*?" Cash demanded.

The detective sighed. "Look, my hands are tied to a certain extent. I have a police department to answer to and laws to follow. A code of conduct, standard operating procedure. I'm sure you're aware," she added, looking at Jack.

Who nodded. Icily.

"I want to hear what you all think Bryan Ferguson and the late Tripp Anthony have to do with Chessa Scott's murder. And next time you think to ask around about anyone, I don't want to hear it from my husband. I want you to come to me or Hart. It is not our goal to arrest the wrong man," she said, looking at Cash pointedly.

Zeke didn't say anything, but he looked over at Cash. Almost like he was asking permission. Which was…a nice thing to do, actually. Cash gave him a nod.

"Carlyle pointed out that it was strange, or at least something worth looking into, that Ferguson was the one who handled Chessa Scott bonding out with Tripp Anthony last year. She's been trying to find a connection between them. And I did last night. Not much to go on, but enough to know they were friendly. Seen together at Rightful Claim more than once."

The detective nodded thoughtfully. "When was the last time they were seen together?"

"It was unclear. Definitely last year before Tripp died, but I couldn't get a time frame."

"Did you make a list of who you spoke to?"

Zeke crossed his arms over his chest. "I didn't ask names."

She waved that away, clearly seeing through Zeke. "I'll want names. Trust me, my husband can give me a list of everyone you spoke with, but it'd be easier if you narrowed it down to the ones who'd seen the two men together. You can email them to me."

Zeke scowled, but the detective didn't seem to notice. "We've looked some into Bryan Ferguson. Just another reason it'd be better if you all came to us. Since Anthony is dead, he wasn't on our list, but he'd been dating Ms. Scott, yes?"

"That was what Chessa said when he bailed her out, according to Ferguson," Jack replied.

The detective nodded. "Does Ferguson know your family has been looking into him?"

Jack shook his head. "I certainly haven't told him or anyone at the department."

"I'm assuming the exception there is…" She trailed off, looked through her notebook. "Deputy Chloe Brink? The one who was questioning the coroner?"

Jack's expression got very hard. "She's looked into some things regarding the murder, but no. She doesn't know we've been looking into Ferguson."

"All right." The detective stood. "I'll have more questions likely, but I'm just going to reiterate that all of this goes a lot smoother if you trust me with what you find. We want the truth as much as you do." She turned her gaze to Cash. "Can you walk me out, Mr. Hudson?"

Cash didn't like that, but he didn't see what choice he had. He squeezed Izzy's hand then released it and stood to follow the detective out.

She didn't say anything until they got to the front door. "You've worked with Bent County before. You and your search dogs?"

Cash nodded, not sure where this was going. "A few years back when there was a missing boy over in the state park."

She nodded. "I read the report. Your dogs found him."

"In the nick of time."

"You've also helped Quinn Peterson at Fool's Gold Investigation."

Cash wasn't sure exactly what the detective knew about that case, what he should be straight about. It felt dangerous to let someone in, someone who thought he was capable of murder.

But she'd given Izzy some consideration and he couldn't ignore that went a long way in his book.

"She was looking for some specific evidence on a case.

Had a scent and an area she thought it might be in, so the dogs searched and found it."

"Yeah. I'd like to do that, Mr. Hudson. But it would be a conflict of interest to tell you why."

"Can't really have my dogs help out if I don't know for what."

"I know, but maybe you have an employee, someone you're not related to, a colleague somewhere else? Who your dogs would listen to?"

"Me."

They both turned to where Carlyle was. Not *hiding* per se, but she had definitely been stealthily following them and listening to that conversation.

The detective sighed. "You have a personal connection to—"

"To who? Your prime suspect?" Carlyle demanded, crossing her arms over her chest, just as Zeke had back there.

"Car."

She turned her slightly belligerent look on him. "Anyone who your dogs will follow, or is qualified to lead your dogs, is going to have a personal connection to you." She turned her attention back to the detective. "I don't think you're bad at your job, Detective, so I think you knew you wouldn't find some random person unconnected to all of this to help you out. And you don't have access to other search dogs, or you wouldn't be asking. So let's not waste time."

"Ms. Daniels—"

"I know how these things go. I can facilitate a search that doesn't discredit your investigation. You wouldn't be here, asking him about his dogs, if you didn't think it could be done."

"You said yourself you're involved with Mr. Hudson.

You're, in fact, his alibi. If you know how this goes, Ms. Daniels, then surely you understand how it looks."

"So, find a way to make it look good," Cash said. Because Carlyle was right. The detective wouldn't be wasting her time with this if she didn't think it could be done. "Carlyle is perfectly capable of handling the search dogs. If I stay out of it, and if you're with her the whole time, and it gets you what you're looking for...isn't it worth the risk that this one little thing doesn't hold up in court?"

She was quiet for a long-drawn-out moment. "Fine. When can you do it?"

"How about now?" Cash and Carlyle asked in unison.

Chapter Eleven

They immediately took the detective down to the dog barn. Carlyle tried not to feel nervous. She'd never taken the dogs off property on her own. She'd never led a full-on, nontraining search on her own.

But they were very carefully not giving away how unqualified Carlyle was to do this while the detective was in earshot.

"So, Carlyle and I will get the dogs loaded up in our Hudson Dog Services truck. We can drive out to the site—"

"You're going to have to stay here, Mr. Hudson."

"I'll stay in the truck and—"

The detective was already shaking her head. "This is already a stretch as is. I can't have you anywhere near the search area. You're going to have to stay here, Mr. Hudson. It's the only way."

Cash didn't look at her, but his expression was clear. He didn't like it.

"Ms. Daniels, I'm going to drive out to the site. I'm going to get everything ready on my end. When you've got the dogs loaded up, text me. I'll text you an address. I'm going to ask you not share that address with anyone. Is this the truck you'll be driving?"

"Yeah."

She noted down the make, model and license plate. "You'll

be cleared to drive up to the site. I'll see you soon." Then she turned and walked back toward the front of the main house where her police cruiser was parked.

Carlyle watched her go with mixed emotions. Then she looked at Cash with even *more* mixed emotions.

His expression was…concerned, she supposed. But not frustrated or angry like she'd expected.

"I can do this," she said, not because she was confident, but because she wanted to assure him. There was just…so much at stake that was *outside* her control. Usually she was only ever risking herself when she was storming through a bad decision.

"I know you can," Cash said, but he was looking at her, still with that concern, like he could *see* the anxiety on her even as she tried to hide it. "The dogs know what they're doing. All you have to do is facilitate. Just like anything else you've done with them. They're the pros. You've been doing this for a year. You know the ropes."

Carlyle nodded, and she knew she was doing a terrible job of keeping the worry off her face because Cash took her by the shoulders, gave them a squeeze. "You can do this. I know you can."

"I know I can." But he saw through her, so why not be honest? Maybe he could temper his expectations if she was. "It's just…a lot of pressure. I don't want to mess it up."

"You can't. All you're doing is taking them out there. Giving them some direction. They're the ones doing the job. If they mess up, Hick just won't get a special treat tonight."

He was trying to make a joke—she knew him well enough he wouldn't deny a dog a treat. But she couldn't force herself to smile or laugh.

"Even if this is a dead end, I'll tell you guys where we

do the search. I don't care what she said. We'll investigate it ourselves later if we have to and—"

Cash shook his head. "It won't be the place. She's testing you. She'll meet you there then take you to a second location."

She hadn't thought of that, but he was right. Of course he was right. The detective wasn't about to make this *easy*.

"Just let the dogs do the work, okay?" Cash said, squeezing her shoulders again. "They'll find what's there, *if* it's there."

Carlyle wasn't so sure about that. If she didn't lead the dogs the right way, she could mess everything up. But this was what had to be done, and she was a *doer*. "I better get going," she said. Because she wanted to keep that worry to herself, not end up blurting it out to him so *he* worried more.

"Be careful. And don't go pissing off the detective just because she's pissing you off."

Carlyle pouted, if only to add some levity to this whole awful situation. "But that's my favorite pastime."

"Try to play this one by the book, Daniels." Then he leaned down and kissed her. And lingered there, his mouth on hers. Unfurling all that warmth and yearning inside of her. Not just a physical yearning, but an ache for something she hadn't let herself want before.

Something she was still too afraid to name, even in the privacy of her own mind. Especially when she was reminded of her run-in with Izzy earlier. She had to warn him lest he walk into that minefield without any preparation.

But part of her was worried he'd drop her like a hot poker. And she wouldn't even be able to blame him. His daughter came first. Should come first.

So, because she was her, she ripped off the bandage. She pulled her mouth away, cleared her throat and tried her best to appear unaffected. "Just FYI, I don't think Izzy is too keen on this whole thing."

"What whole thing?"

"The...us thing. Not like she thinks something's going on. Just that I think she picked up on my feelings for you, and she made it clear I should steer myself elsewhere."

His eyebrows furrowed. "She loves you."

"Yeah, but... She loves you more. The best and most. Sharing you is a pretty new concept. She's not a fan."

"I'll talk to her."

Carlyle immediately shook her head. "Look, this isn't my business, I know that, but you can't go *talk* to her after she warns me off. Then she thinks I'm some whiny tattletale. And that doesn't help anyone." Least of all Carlyle herself. It would just kill her if Izzy suddenly stopped trusting her.

"I'm going to have to talk to her anyway, Car. I'm not sneaking around pretending this isn't happening."

Oh, how her traitorous, silly little heart fluttered at that. "Okay, fine, but don't mention me. Don't mention not liking it. And when she tells you she doesn't, you listen. You can kick me to the curb over it." She was talking too fast, saying too much, but she couldn't quite stop herself. "No hard feelings. Just be straight with me, okay? No...beating around the bush or trying to make it nice. Just straight out."

He looked so...concerned. She didn't know what to do with that reaction. She wanted to run in the opposite direction. She didn't want...concern. She was tough. She was brave. She was...

He reached out and cupped her face in his hands. She was *toast*.

"My daughter dictates a lot of parts of my life, and rightfully so, but not everything," he said, so very seriously. "I still have to...be able... She can't dictate everything without any discussion. Without getting to the heart of it. That isn't fair to me and it's not raising my daughter the right way to let her just…always gets what she wants."

"You're going to keep…whatever we're doing…even if she hates it? Hates me because of it? Hates you because of it?" Carlyle didn't want that. As much as she wanted *him*, she didn't want that.

"I'm going to talk to her, Carlyle. Because there's no reason for her to not like me having a relationship with you—which is what we're doing. It might be uncomfortable for her at first, for all of us. It's new, and I don't expect it to be easy. But she doesn't get to decide wholesale. It has to be a discussion."

"And if after you've discussed it, she's still against it?"

"Let's take it one step at a time, Car. Like, step one. Go find this evidence the detective wants."

Carlyle wrinkled her nose. "What if it hurts your case?"

Cash sighed, dropped his hands. He looked out at where the detective had gone. "Did you see her when she looked at Izzy?"

"Yeah, she wanted her gone, but then when Izzy spoke up for herself, she gave her an out. Treated her like…a whole person, not just a kid to be shunted off. It was good."

"I wanted to take against her for having me on her list, but she's doing her due diligence. She also didn't stop Zeke last night, when it's clear her husband gave her the opportunity to. She's not telling us to butt out. She's bringing us even more in. Maybe it'll bite me in the ass, but I think I trust her."

Carlyle blew out a breath. "Yeah, I do too. But I don't trust this *whole thing*. Something's off and I don't like it."

"Agreed. All we can do is take it one step at a time." He tucked a strand of hair behind her ear, waited until she met his gaze. "Be careful, Car," he said seriously.

She'd never spent much time being careful, but she figured now was a good time to start. So, she smiled. "I will be."

CASH HAD BEEN forced to have a lot of tough conversations with his daughter over the years. Between everything with Chessa, to the danger the Hudsons routinely dealt in, to Anna getting pregnant *before* she was married to Hawk and where *did* babies come from then, to—quite frankly, the worst—puberty.

He hadn't done a good job every time, but he'd tried. If there was anything he'd had to accept in being a parent, it was that the best you could do was *try*, and if your trying sucked, you just had to get better. Lean on his family a little bit.

So, as Cash—plagued by uncertainty—walked toward the dog barn with his daughter, knowing he had to have this potentially difficult conversation, he realized it was not anything new.

But it *was* a new subject. Him being involved with someone. Finding the right balance between including Izzy and not letting her think she got to make his decisions *for* him. They were a family, but some things were private. Someday, she'd want to date, and he doubted very much he'd have a say.

He wanted to go jump off the nearest mountain at the thought.

"Can we work with the horses again today?" Izzy asked, swinging her arms in the pretty morning like she didn't have a care in the world. He wished she could always feel that way, particularly after this morning's breakfast.

"Well, technically it's Crew Three's turn, and Carlyle had to take them with her to work with the detective this morning." They should take Crew Two out on the trail, but

Cash wanted this whole murder thing solved before they went too far from home base. "What if we take the puppies through the obstacle course instead?"

"Pita too?"

"I'll text Hawk." He pulled out his phone and texted Hawk to send his dog out. None of them were puppies anymore, but until they had a new batch, they'd be known as the puppies.

"Before you get the rest of them out, I want to talk to you about something."

All the ease and happiness leaked out of her quickly. Her arms slumped and she shaded her eyes to look up at him.

"Nothing bad happened. This is a good thing I want to talk to you about, I like to think." He crouched to make himself eye level, though it wasn't much of a crouch anymore. She was going to be a tall one, and that ache of too much joy and wistfulness wrapped around his heart like it always did.

But that frown did not leave Izzy's face. She watched him with deep, deep suspicion as he tried to come up with the words.

He knew he should start out quickly, so she didn't invent terrible scenarios in her head, but he was struggling to find the words to start. "Iz... You... You like Carlyle."

Her frown deepened. Which wasn't exactly expected, but maybe it should have been with what Carlyle had told him.

"So?" she said, a little belligerently.

"So. I...like her too,"

"She works for you."

"Yes, and she's a...friend."

"Cool," Izzy said, trying to turn away from him, but he reached out for her arm, kept her in place. Because her *cool* sounded anything but.

"I like her a lot, actually," he said firmly. Because he could interrogate Izzy's feelings on the matter instead of be clear about his own, but that felt like a bit of a cop-out. He'd already initiated this relationship with Carlyle. He wasn't going back on it. No matter how she'd assured him he *could*.

She had heartbreak in her eyes like no one had ever chosen her over anything. And maybe they hadn't, and he couldn't *choose* her over Izzy, but this wasn't…so cut-and-dried. Life never was. It wasn't about *choosing* over anyone else.

It was just life.

"As more than a friend," he continued, while Izzy scowled at him. "I wanted to let you know that."

"What? That she's suddenly your girlfriend?" Izzy said, with the snotty kind of look that usually irritated him.

He was not an old man, but man, the word *girlfriend* made him feel old and out of place. Still, it was a word that made sense to Izzy. No matter how snottily she'd said it.

"Yeah. You seem to have a problem with that. Which I have to say, I don't understand because I know you love her."

"Yeah, I do." She jerked her arm away from him. "Because she's *my* friend," Izzy said, exploding. "She's on *my* side. Finally, there's someone who doesn't listen to *you*. She listened to *me*. She cared about *me*." Izzy spun around and pointed at him. "Now…she's yours. And she'll listen to *you*."

There was a well of anger there that he hadn't anticipated. That he didn't know what to do with. But beyond just not understanding, her words hit at just about every little insecurity he had. "Izzy… Do you really think I don't listen? I don't care?"

Her face got all crumpled looking, like right before she cried. But before he could reach out for her, she stomped away from him. Not far. Just to the entrance of the barn.

"I just…"

Cash didn't know if she didn't have the words, or just couldn't squeeze them out. So he found some of his own to give her.

"You are the most important thing in my world. You always will be. I know I'm not perfect, but I know if I've made anything clear to you, it's that. That doesn't mean I don't have other important things. I always have. We are very lucky to have a big family, getting bigger every year, who we love and loves us back. They're all important."

Izzy turned very slowly. If she'd let any tears fall, she'd wiped them away first. "You love her?" she asked, her voice wavery and those tears still visible in her eyes, even if they didn't fall.

What was with everyone asking him that question? "I don't…know."

"Shouldn't you?"

"It's just complicated. Adult relationships aren't so cut-and-dried. And there are…extenuating circumstances." And now he just wished he could reverse time and *not* do this here. Or anywhere. Ever.

Izzy swallowed. "Everything keeps changing."

And how. "I know, baby. I can't promise you that'll stop. Life is change. You're going to grow up on me. And you're going to make your own decisions, and I don't have to like them. Though I hope I will. But I can promise… Nothing comes in front of you for me, Iz. And if we talk about it, we can work through whatever comes."

She looked down at the ground, and he knew she was trying so hard not to cry. "I just… Aunt Mary is going to have a baby, and she won't have time for me like she used to. You'll spend time with Carlyle, just like all the aunts and uncles… Except Jack." She looked up at him, all those tears making her blue eyes bluer. "Where do I fit if you all get married and have babies?"

He pulled her into his chest, and she didn't push him away. "You fit right here, baby. Because you are my baby. You're our first baby here on this ranch. Nothing changes that. Not more kids, not more people. You'll *always* be ours. Long before everyone else."

She leaned her head on his shoulder, and he felt the tell-tale tears seeping through his shirt. He rubbed her back, tried to find the words to ease this change in the midst of all this danger.

"You'll help with Mary's baby. Just like you're doing with Caroline. And...just think. You're going to middle school in the fall. There will be sports and clubs and all sorts of things." Things he'd always been leery about letting her join, but he clearly needed to...let go. Find a way to give her a bigger life, not a smaller one.

"I know it's hard to feel like everything is changing around you, but it's just...life moving along. You add people, you lose people." He pulled her back, so she had to look at him. "But nothing ever changes that you're part of this." He pointed out at the ranch, at the main house—where Pita was racing across the yard toward them. "Love just expands, baby. It's not something that can get used up."

She took a deep, shaky breath. "Chessa... She stopped loving me. She used it all up and then there was nothing left."

Cash wished there was some way to heal that wound, but he'd had to accept that he couldn't. Only time and growing up and being there for her could. Or maybe he just hoped it could.

"Your mom never loved much beyond herself. There are probably some reasons why that was, but I could never get to the heart of them. I tried, but… Nothing that Chessa ever felt or didn't, did or didn't, is about you. Nothing. And I know it might be hard to believe that, and maybe you can't just yet. But I want you to look at *all* the people who are here and think about them and their place in your life. Not the one person who isn't."

Izzy swallowed. "I just…don't want things to change. I want Carlyle to be my friend and…"

"She will be. Whatever is going on between Carlyle and me at any time isn't ever going to be about how you guys feel about each other. And I think you know Carlyle well enough to know she's not afraid of making me mad. She loves you, independently of me. She sticks up for you when she thinks it's right, because she's been in very similar shoes. That doesn't change just because we…date," he finished lamely. "I promise."

She let out a long breath, then nodded. "Okay. I guess… I guess it's okay then."

Cash didn't point out he hadn't been asking for permission, because it was nice to have. Because having her blessing meant something. "I love you, Iz. Nothing ever in a million years changes that. Nothing."

She curled into him, holding on tight. "I love you too, Dad."

Pita arrived with delighted yips and barks, jumping in between them with enthusiasm. Izzy laughed and released Cash to throw her arms around Pita and wrestle with him a bit. And for a moment, Cash let himself forget about murder, and Carlyle out on a search job, and the hole Chessa had left in his daughter's heart.

And just enjoyed the moment.

Chapter Twelve

Carlyle pulled up to the address the detective had texted her. Like Cash had said, it clearly wasn't the end location. The detective was alone, standing next to her police cruiser, in a kind of abandoned parking lot outside of Bent.

The detective held up her hand in a wave. Her other hand held a cell phone to her ear. Carlyle went ahead and parked and got out of the van, then took a surreptitious look around.

This location wasn't in the boundaries of the town of Bent, but it was close. The saloon Zeke had cased the other night couldn't be more than a mile or two away from this spot.

"Did you look under the potty stool?" the detective was saying into her phone.

Carlyle raised an eyebrow. What the hell was a *potty stool*?

"That's where I found it last time. I have to go. Yeah. Love you too, bye." She hit a button on her phone and pocketed it, smiling at Carlyle. "Sorry. Family emergency."

"A lot of potty stool-related emergencies?"

The detective laughed. "I have three kids under the age of six. So, yes."

Carlyle blinked. It was hard to imagine this very professional and with-it detective with *three* little kids. Not to mention, Carlyle had been to Rightful Claim, the bar the detective's husband owned. She knew what he looked like. "You're really married to that hot, tattooed saloon guy?"

"Yep."

"That's really hard to believe." She remembered Cash's words to not irritate the detective a little too late.

But the detective didn't get offended. She didn't even frown. She grinned. "Oh, Ms. Daniels, you have *no* idea." Then she pointed to Carlyle's truck. "Am I okay to ride with you in the truck to the search site?"

"Allergic to dogs?"

"No."

"Then you're good to go." Carlyle thought about bringing up the fact this wasn't how the detective said it would go, but then she decided to just roll with it. Let the detective dictate how this would go and just observe.

A woman could glean a lot just from observing. If she could keep her big mouth shut. Well, she'd *try*.

"Once we're inside the truck, I'm going to turn my body cam on. That way, we've got everything documented should we need it for a trial. Once we get to the site, Hart and two other Bent County deputies will be there. We've got the search area blocked off."

"And something for the dogs to use to search off of, I assume?"

"When we get there. Everything is going to go on camera. The more transparent we can be, the better off we'll be come trial."

"You keep talking about a trial, but we don't even have a suspect yet." The detective said *nothing*. "I thought we were working together."

"We are, Ms. Daniels. Believe it or not, I don't want to arrest Mr. Hudson. Off the record? I don't think he did it, and it's a waste of time trying to pin it on him."

"On the record?" Carlyle asked, because she wasn't dumb enough to be swayed by a little good cop, even without the presence of a bad cop.

"We're exploring every possible and reasonable avenue," she said, sounding very formal and official.

Carlyle really didn't want to like her, but she was making it hard. "Well, let's go find something for the record then."

The detective nodded. "Just remember. We're recording *everything*." She patted the little attachment to her police vest.

Carlyle nodded, appreciating the clarity. No attempt to get her to say something dumb and incriminating on camera. They got in the truck, and the dogs whined a little bit at the newcomer, but they were well trained enough to stay put.

The detective gave directions as Carlyle drove. They passed Rightful Claim, rounded the corner and entered the back alley.

Where Zeke had been *poking around*, as the detective had called it this morning. Carlyle didn't say anything about it. With the camera running, she figured it best she said as little as possible.

The detective got out, so Carlyle did too. Detective Hart and two uniformed deputies were waiting, and there was an area of the alley and the building behind the saloon sectioned off with crime-scene tape.

"The area taped off is what we're searching," Detective Delaney-Carson explained as they walked over to the other officers.

"What do you have for the dogs to get a scent?"

Hart produced a plastic bag. Inside was a torn scrap of fabric. Carlyle figured the streak of brown on the gray-and-pink fabric was blood. Chessa's blood.

She set that thought away as best she could.

"We can go in this building through that open door, but only the ground floor. They can also search around out here within the tape, but not beyond."

"I'll have to be the one who gives the scent to them," Carlyle said, which wasn't *exactly* true, but true enough. "They won't understand what they're supposed to do if it's any of you. You'll also want to stand out of the way and remain mostly still so they're not distracted by you. I've got six dogs. They'll take turns in teams of two. When they're out in the field, you want to just stay out of their way."

"What if they want to go beyond the borders of the search?" one of the officers asked.

"I'll stop them." Carlyle looked around the blocked off area. It seemed such an odd location to be cordoned off. Had Chessa been found here? She glanced around, looking for security cameras, but didn't see any. "What if they hit on something beyond the borders? Can't I just let them go for it?"

"We don't have a search warrant for any area beyond," Detective Delaney-Carson said. "The street is fine, but inside or around certain buildings is private property. But if they're pointing to that area, we can work on expanding our search warrant with that due cause. So, you'll just let us know and we'll go from there."

Carlyle didn't know what to think of that, but she supposed it was just something to file away. Maybe Jack would have an idea what it meant and why.

She moved to the truck and unleashed the first two dogs. She prepped them for the search, then took the bag of evidence from Hart and opened it. Then she let the dogs do their thing. She followed them, and Detective Delaney-Carson followed her. The other three stayed where they were in different corners, patrolling the area so no one happened upon them, Carlyle guessed.

Both dogs immediately went for the building. Carlyle shared a look with Detective Delaney-Carson then followed the dogs. The detective kept right by Carlyle's side, then stopped her before she entered the building.

"We already gave it a sweep, but we can't go upstairs, so let me go first."

Carlyle nodded and the woman drew her gun and went in first. Carlyle followed her in. The dogs sniffed around the empty room. More like a warehouse than anything. All concrete and grimy windows, which let in a little light but not much visibility. The detective kept her weapon drawn, but she motioned Carlyle forward.

There was definitely something going on here that Carlyle hadn't been let in on, and she didn't know what to make of that. She figured it wasn't malicious, but that didn't mean it didn't make her nervous.

Carlyle watched as the dogs headed for the stairs.

"You can't let them go up there," the detective said.

Carlyle gave the order to stop, and both dogs sat obediently. Right there at the bottom of the stairs.

"You sure they can't go upstairs?"

"You have reason to believe they scent something upstairs?"

Carlyle pointed to both of them, sitting at attention, waiting for the okay signal. "Clearly."

The detective nodded. She pulled her radio to her mouth. "Hart. The dogs want upstairs. Call it in. See if someone can expand that search warrant for us."

The return came back staticky but affirmative. The detective still held her gun, her eyes focused on the stairs. She had a frown on her face.

She wanted up there. She *suspected* something up there.

Carlyle wondered if she could just…go. She wasn't a cop. Search warrants didn't matter to her. But then one of the dogs let out two low *woofs*. Carlyle frowned. It wasn't one of the normal search responses, but she thought Cash had told her something about that indication one time. A long time ago. When he'd first been introducing her to all the dogs.

She looked at the dog who'd made the noise. Colby. Colby hadn't always been search and rescue. Or she had, but it had been for something else… What was it?

When Carlyle remembered, her body went a little cold. "Detective, I think we better get out of here."

"Why?"

"These dogs are trained for search and rescue, but this one in particular also has some training with finding drugs, weapons and explosives." Carlyle didn't know the exact signs for all of those, but she knew the dog's reaction just… wasn't good.

"All right."

Carlyle signaled the dogs out of the building, she and the detective following. But just as they reached the door-way something…exploded. Loud and bright, and then the ceiling rained down on them.

Hot. Bright. *Hell.* Something—or *somethings*—crashed on top of her. Painful, but nothing heavy or sharp enough to do real damage. She hoped.

The dogs were out, and Carlyle was about to jump forward to follow them, but she heard swearing and looked behind her. The detective was on the ground, conscious, but when she tried to get up, she swore even harder and didn't manage. That's when Carlyle noticed she had something stuck in her leg.

But worse, all around them were flames. The entire upstairs had exploded and collapsed, and none of the sounds the fire and building were making could be good. The roof was crumbling. Carlyle had to get them out of here. She grabbed the detective's arm. "This might hurt, but it's better than staying put." Then she dragged her out through the doorway.

They'd likely sustained some burns, and if the blood dripping on the ground was anything to go by, she had a bit of a head wound. And *maybe* dragging the detective was hell on her stitches from the other day. But she was on her own two feet and of sound mind.

She managed to drag the detective away from the flames. She thought—hoped—she heard sirens in the distance but mostly it was just the crackle and creak of a building going up in flames.

Carlyle kept dragging Laurel, but she was running out of steam. She managed to make it around the corner before she stumbled a little bit and fell on her butt. She scooted her back against the brick building and the detective did the same.

"Well, thanks. Probably saved my life, Ms. Daniels."

"Any time."

"Your head's bleeding."

"Yeah, so's your leg. Don't look at it," Carlyle immediately told her, because the giant piece of debris sticking out of the woman's leg was about to cause Carlyle to lose her lunch, and she'd seen worse, she liked to think.

But yikes.

"Don't worry. Been hurt once or twice. Know the drill." But the detective closed her eyes, leaned her head against the wall. Then she swore. Loudly. "This better not put me off the damn case."

Hart came running up to them, crouched in front of the detective, worry all over him. "You okay?"

"Yeah, thanks to her."

"Paramedics are on their way with fire, plus another unit." Hart looked at the detective's leg, blanched, swallowed, but didn't shake or faint. He looked over at Carlyle. "Anything beside that gash on your head?"

The old stab wound throbbed, but she didn't think that was relevant. Besides, her heart was beating too hard, and her limbs were too shaky to really take stock. "No. Where are my dogs?"

"They ran straight for the truck, so we leashed them up with the others. That okay?"

Carlyle nodded. She didn't want to have to tell Cash what happened. "Yeah, listen. I better get them back to the ranch." Of course she felt about as sturdy as a dead tree branch, but no one needed to know that.

"No. You'll get checked out. Sit tight. I've got some phone calls to make. Do you want to call someone from the ranch to come pick up the dogs?"

Carlyle nodded. "I left my phone in the truck though."

"Use mine," Detective Delaney-Carson said, holding out her cell phone, but before Carlyle could make the call, the detective grabbed Hart by the pants' leg.

"Hart," the detective said, sounding like she was trying to be more firm than she actually *sounded* firm. "Don't you dare call my husband."

"Grady'll kill me if I don't."

"Yeah, well. The price you pay for being my partner, I guess. He'll find out soon enough, hopefully once I'm all bandaged up. You tell him now? *I* kill you."

But there wasn't any more to say because an ambulance pulled up. One EMT went straight for the detective and one for Carlyle. They poked and prodded at her head, asked her too many questions to count. And fully ignored her when she said she was fine.

"We'll transport you both to the hospital in the same ambulance. Easier that way. You need a stretcher, Detective. Ms. Daniels, you can walk on your own accord if you feel up to it."

Carlyle nodded, then steeled herself to look at the detective. But they'd removed the debris and there was bloody gauze over her thigh.

She was conscious though. Talking to the EMT with the stretcher, every bit the in-charge detective even after what had happened.

What *had* happened?

Carlyle got one last glimpse of the building. Something had exploded on that top floor they weren't allowed in. And that was fishy. But the detective had been acting weird. Like she knew something she wasn't letting on.

Once they were all loaded up in the ambulance, Carlyle didn't make her phone call. She looked at the detective. "That thing off?" she said, pointing to the body cam.

The woman reached up, switched something on it. "Now it is."

"Detective, you know what happened in there, don't you?"

"I think you earned the right to call me Laurel. And maybe be the namesake of our next kid."

"Jeez. Isn't three enough?"

"We make cute babies."

It *almost* made Carlyle laugh. "I bet."

The detective—*Laurel*—sighed. "We have some theories. I'll tell you about it. Make your phone call first."

WHEN CASH'S PHONE RANG, he didn't recognize the number, but with Carlyle off searching for things with his dogs, he couldn't just ignore it. So he answered, with a pit of dread in his stomach. "Hello?"

"Hey."

"This isn't your number."

"No, it's the detective's. I'm helping her out with something, but we've got to leave the dogs behind. Can you come pick them up? Detective Hart will have the truck and the dogs at the Sheriff's Office."

"What are you working on?" Cash asked.

"I can't explain just yet. I will tonight though, promise."

"Carl—"

"Really, Cash. It's fine. I promise. We just need the dogs picked up. I'll be home tonight, and I'll be able to explain everything. Just too many…people around right now. Okay?"

He didn't like this at all, but he understood why she might not be able to talk. But then why not text? "You sure you're okay?"

She laughed, and *that* sounded more like her. "Yeah, I'm sure. If I was in some kind of trouble, I'd be too busy fighting my way out of it to call you."

Fair enough, even though the idea made him frown. "Okay, I'll come pick up the truck. Zeke's still out here, he can drop me off. He was talking about doing some more poking around Bent anyway."

"Oh, he doesn't need to do that."

"Why not?"

"Listen, I've got lots of stuff to tell you guys, but can you just stay away from Bent for now? It's not dangerous, I promise. I just want to make sure we aren't messing with this case. That detective was right. We need to make sure she can build a case."

Now he was *really* worried. "Carlyle, I have never once heard you admit someone else was right."

"I didn't say the *male* detective was right. Then you'd really have to worry."

Which was fair enough, and almost made him want to laugh if he could around the little weight of worry in his stomach. But she was a grown woman, and everything she said made *sense*, even if it didn't land right.

"Just get the dogs back to the ranch," she said. "I'll call you when I need a ride if I can't hitch one home with one of the cops."

"Car..." He couldn't get over the feeling she was holding out on him. That something was *wrong*. But she'd called the ranch...home, and that felt...important. "All right. Just promise you'll call. And come home soon."

"I promise. By dinner. Get the dogs. We'll talk soon. Bye."

"Bye." He pulled the phone away from his ear, trying to tell himself everything was fine. If there was a problem, she would have at least hinted at one. She'd only hide something to protect him, and he couldn't think of what she'd be protecting him from.

But he was damn well taking Zeke with him. First, he hunted down Mary to make sure she'd keep Izzy within someone's eyesight at all times. Then he found Zeke and explained the phone call.

"Since when is she about listening to detectives' orders?"

"I don't know," Cash said. "I don't like it."

"Yeah, me neither," Zeke said. "All right. Ready?"

Cash nodded, but before they could make way for the door, Hawk entered the room with a phone to his ear. He made a stopping motion to them, and though Cash felt impatience snapping, he waited. And so did Zeke.

When Hawk finally pulled the phone away from his ear, his expression was blank. Cop blank. "I just got called into a fire. There was an explosion. One Bent County detective and one civilian were hurt and taken to the hospital."

Cash was already moving—and so was Zeke, swearing a blue streak.

"You can't just go tearing off—" Hawk called after them, but they were outside and in Zeke's truck before he finished.

"Hold on," Zeke muttered, and then he drove like a bat out of hell for the hospital.

Cash only wished he'd go faster.

Chapter Thirteen

Carlyle managed to downplay her injuries to the nurse. There was enough confusion that she didn't even have to take her shirt off. They just cleaned up her head—no stitches this time—and let her go with a little printout about painkillers and what to look for.

Carlyle knew she should head out. Call Cash to pick her up. Or maybe call Chloe so she didn't have to tell Cash about this at all. Maybe if she took off the bandage before she got back to the ranch, he wouldn't even know.

But she hadn't gotten much out of Laurel about what the detective knew in the short ambulance ride, and Carlyle was determined to return to the ranch with more information than when she'd left.

So, she poked around the hospital until she figured out where Laurel had gone—she'd had to be admitted due to the severity of her injury. Carlyle waited until the hallway was empty and no one appeared to be in her room, then slipped in.

Laurel looked up from where she'd been messing with the IV in her arm and frowned a little at Carlyle. "Are you supposed to be in here?"

"Are you supposed to be trying to take that IV out?"

"That is *not* what I was doing."

"Uh-huh."

"You get the green light or are you sneaking off?"

"Green light. Just a little scrape on my head," she said, pointing to her bandage and ignoring the throbbing pain in her side. "You need surgery?"

"Still some discussion on that. I'll riot," she muttered irritably. And since Carlyle understood the feeling so well, she smiled.

"No one out there?" Laurel asked, jerking her chin toward the door.

Carlyle shook her head. "Pretty empty."

"Okay, come here so I can talk softly. I don't think anyone would be listening, but we're not going to be too careful with small towns where everyone knows everyone. Pull up that chair."

Carlyle did as she was told and was grateful when Laurel didn't beat around the bush.

"I'm going to tell you a few things. I shouldn't name names, but I'm going to because your people probably need to be on the lookout, and because I don't know how long I'll be stuck here. Hart will keep working on your case, and he's as good as me. I should leave it at that, but I figure you and yours will poke around anyway, so why not poke in the right direction?"

"That sounds very un-cop of you."

Laurel smiled. "I would have been highly insulted by that when I first started out, but these days, I'll take it as a compliment. I feel like we're on the cusp of something. It's complicated, and I haven't been able to untie all the little knots yet. But there's a correlation between Bryan Ferguson, Tripp Anthony and Butch Scott."

Carlyle hadn't heard of Butch before, but Scott was Chessa's last name.

"Chessa's brother," Laurel confirmed. "Half-brother,

anyway, according to his birth certificate. And Butch's step-mother owned that building across from Rightful Claim. Where we found Chessa's body. Butch and Bryan were step-siblings once upon a time, and Butch, Bryan and Tripp all graduated high school together. Not uncommon out here, and I haven't gotten far enough to know if they were ever friends, kept being friends, but the ownership of that build-ing was suspect."

"Even more so now."

"Yeah."

"Look, Hart will keep tugging on the line. I might need a day or two to talk my way around doctors and my hus-band to get back on the case, but we're not going anywhere. We're going to solve this."

The door flew open. "Speak of the devil," Laurel mut-tered. "Run. Hide. Save yourself."

The man did look a bit like a devil. He was *very* large, one arm nearly covered in tattoos. He had a beard, and his hair was a little wild. He looked like he would tear down the foundations of the earth, and Carlyle had enough expe-rience with men—particularly the protective sort—to see it was about the fact his wife had been hurt, and there was nothing he could do about it. So he was just going to be... loudly and impotently angry about it.

"What are you doing here?" the detective—*Laurel*—demanded of the man who was her husband. "You are sup-posed to be on kid duty."

"And now your sister is. What the hell, princess?"

Princess? People really did have secret lives you couldn't guess at.

"Grady, this is Carlyle. Carlyle, my husband."

"Don't pull that polite BS with me," the man grumbled

as he strode to the other side of Laurel's hospital bed, but he looked over at Carlyle and gave her a nod. "Hi."

"Hey."

"I assume the two guys yelling in the waiting room who I used as a diversion belong to you."

Carlyle blinked. *Two* men. Her brothers? Well, no reason to feel bummed about that. She *had* lied to Cash about where she was. Well. Only sorta. She was fine. Cleared and on her way out.

But apparently, first she had to deal with her brothers and how they'd gotten wind of her situation. "I guess I should go...put a stop to that."

But the man's attention was already back on his wife, and Carlyle could still see all that anger, but she could also see the gentle way he took Laurel's hand, and that anger was just love and worry all tangled up in something that might feel useful.

She supposed that's what married people with three kids who wanted another one did. Carlyle didn't know what to do with the weird feeling in her gut, so she went to find her brothers.

But it wasn't them out at the nurse's station yelling. Well, one of the angry men in the waiting room was. The other one was Cash.

It was an odd realization, to see some of that violent anger in his eyes that had been in the detective's husband's. Like she might matter to him *that* much.

And something inside of her—something she'd shored up so many times in her life, plugged all the cracks and holes, fought tooth and nail to keep it intact—came crumbling down.

The tears spilled over, and she walked over to Cash. Her breathing hitched, and she didn't want to sob, but she was a little afraid that noise that came out of her was exactly that. As he turned, he frowned, but pulled her into his arms.

She supposed it was all of it. Explosions and tangled webs of people they hadn't figured out. Cash in her bed and Izzy's not-so-subtle disapproval. That look in his eyes. The detective and potty chairs and tattooed husbands and debris sticking out of her leg, all because she wanted to find the truth.

God, Carlyle was so tired of people getting hurt to find the truth. Her whole life. The *whole* of it.

"Hey." She heard the surprise in Cash's voice, but he held her there, tight and close, rubbing a comforting hand up and down her back. "It's okay. You're okay," he murmured.

And the silly thing was, she knew that, but it made everything better when he said it.

IN A TURN of events Cash didn't quite know what to do with, Zeke handed him the keys to his truck. "You take her home. I'll get the dogs."

Cash had figured he'd have to fight him on it. Zeke was the more formidable brother, mostly because Mary had Walker wrapped around her little finger. Walker had been threaded into the Hudson family and ranch life. Zeke kept himself apart.

But this was an acknowledgement of…something. So, Cash handed the keys to the dog truck over to Zeke. He had a million admonitions to offer about how to drive with the dogs, how to leash them properly, how to make everything okay.

But in the end, he offered none. Zeke would figure it out. The important thing was getting Carlyle back to the ranch where she could rest. The woman was *crying*, despite the fact she was on her own two feet and seemed to be okay.

Carlyle sniffled into his shoulder, then gradually pulled herself back. Zeke put his hand on her shoulder, and she looked over at him.

"You really okay, kid?" he asked, with a gentleness Cash had never heard out of him.

She nodded. Didn't give her brother a hard time for calling her *kid*. Cash and Zeke exchanged a worried look over her head, but what was there to do?

Zeke left and Cash led Carlyle back out to the parking lot. He'd never seen her cry like that, never expected to. She brazened through everything, and he knew there were deeper feelings under all that bravado, but he hadn't expected a...breakdown, he supposed.

They climbed into Zeke's truck without saying a word. She'd stopped crying, but the evidence of it was all over her face. He'd *planned* on chewing her out for not telling them what was going on, but now he didn't have the heart to. So he just...drove.

She laid her head on his shoulder the whole way back. She didn't say anything, and while he occasionally opened his mouth to say something, in the end, he just kept it shut. Sometimes, comfortable silence was the best medicine.

When he pulled up to a stop in front of the ranch, he made a move to get out, but Carlyle didn't. She just sat there staring at the house.

"Everything okay?"

She didn't look at him, but she answered his question. "You haven't even been mad about me not telling you the truth."

"You seem upset enough without me adding to it."

"That's nice."

"Is it?"

She finally looked over. "Yeah. Because I probably would have been a jerk about it if the situation was reversed."

"I'm beginning to think you're a big old softy, Carlyle. And not a jerk at all."

She let out a little huff of a sound, *almost* a laugh. "That's nice that you think that."

"That's me. Mr. Nice."

"But you're hot too, if it makes you feel better."

It was his turn to laugh. She was sounding more and more like herself, even if he didn't know what to do with that. "You need some rest. I assume they gave you instructions for dealing with that?" he said, finally addressing the bandage on her head.

"Yeah, in my pocket."

"So, we'll go take care of it."

"I need to tell everyone some stuff Laurel, the detective, told me. About the case, about the connections."

"Come on, Car. You're beat."

"Yeah, but the detective who was on your side is in the hospital, and I have information that we should be looking at." She leaned toward him, across the center console. So serious, so...*worried*. "Being beat can take a back seat." She pushed herself out of the truck, hopped down before he could rush around to stop her.

He frowned. "You have to take care of yourself."

"If there's anything I've learned, it's sometimes the only way to take care of yourself is to see the damn thing through so it can stop hanging over your head. This is too big to tip-toe around. We've got to dive in, no matter how we feel."

If nothing else, she was back to her normal go-getting self, but... That was not him. Not anymore. He'd left all that *dive in* thinking behind when Izzy came along. But that was the extreme again.

Maybe what the two of them needed most from each other was the balancing act. The compromise. "All right. We'll compromise. I'll get Jack and whoever else is within reach right now. Get this over with. Anyone who doesn't make it, Jack will spread the info. You've got fifteen minutes, then you're in bed. And you're going to hand over those instructions."

She frowned, but she eventually slid the paper out of her pocket as they entered the house.

"Sit," he said, pointing to the couch. "I'll be right back."

He went through the house, found Jack, Anna with Caroline on her hip, and Walker standing in the kitchen over a pan of brownies.

"She's in the living room," Cash told Walker before he could make the angry demand that was clearly on the tip of his tongue.

Walker left quickly.

"Where's Iz?"

"She and Mary are up in Mary's room going over nursery colors," Anna said. "It's keeping her occupied. What's going on? Zeke already called and said Carlyle's okay."

"Come on out to the living room. Carlyle will explain. Anyone else around?"

Jack shook his head. "Palmer and Louisa are up at their house site. Grant and Dahlia are still out visiting her sister. Hawk's dealing with the fire."

"We'll do this just us then. Fill in everyone else after the fact."

"Hawk should be home soon," Anna said. "We can needle him for more information on the fire."

Cash nodded as they walked out to the living room. Walker sat next to Carlyle, who was rolling her eyes. A good sign, Cash thought.

Once everyone got situated, Carlyle jumped right into it. "Did any of you know Chessa's brother?"

"Chessa only has sisters," Cash replied.

"Laurel said—"

"You're on a first-name basis with the detective now?" Walker interrupted suspiciously.

"Yeah, saved her life and all."

"Jesus," Cash and Walker said in unison.

But Cash couldn't think about lives in danger. He had to focus on the problem at hand. "Chessa doesn't have a brother." *Didn't* have a brother, he reminded himself internally. Because she was gone this time. Really gone. Such a strange ribbon of grief and relief every day over that, and he wasn't sure he'd ever fully come to terms with it. Which made him think of Izzy upstairs with Mary, worried about how things would change, how she would fit. Knowing the answer had never been Chessa, and now never could be.

"Laurel said it was a half-brother. And this half-brother's stepmother owned the building that exploded."

As if on cue with the word *exploded*, Hawk came in.

"What can you tell us?" Anna demanded.

"Not much, yet. Sent some things away to be tested." He took Caroline from Anna, kissed the baby's head. "What I can say is, the explosion set at the building Carlyle and the detective were searching was deliberate."

"Obviously," Carlyle muttered.

"And we…found some human remains in the debris."

An echo of shock went through the room, and Cash was glad Izzy wasn't here to hear that. Maybe she'd have to know eventually, but for right now they could stick to one murder.

"We'll do some tests there too. Determine if the fire was the cause of death or something before."

"I don't think it was the fire," Carlyle said. "The detective and I were in the building. I think the police were in and out of the building before I got there. They only had a search warrant for the downstairs, but… We would have heard someone upstairs. The dogs would have sensed someone upstairs, right?"

She looked at Cash, so he nodded. "They might not have reacted to it though, if they were searching for the scent."

Hawk nodded. "It's all good information to have. The police are tracking down the property owner. Luckily, they already had contact with her regarding the search warrant so it's just a matter of finding her. I've done what I can do today in terms of the fire. Now, it's a bit of a waiting game until tests come back and more questioning is done."

"There's more though. This half brother you guys apparently didn't know about, Butch Scott—"

"Butch Scott. Wait. We know Butch Scott. I thought they were…cousins or something?" Anna said, looking at Cash.

"That's what she always told us."

"Maybe he was," Carlyle said, as if this strange mistake didn't mean anything. "More important, Butch Scott and Bryan Ferguson were stepbrothers at one point."

All eyes turned to Jack. His expression was not as cop-cool as Cash had expected it to be.

"I had some news of my own I wanted to share once we got everyone together. Bryan didn't show up for work tonight. No one knows where he went." He looked up at Hawk. "Do you have any more information on that corpse in your building?"

Hawk took a breath. "The initial consensus is adult male, but most identifying characteristics had been burned away. Until the tests are run. One happenstance missing person doesn't mean it'll be Bryan."

"But it could be," Jack said firmly.

Hawk nodded. "Yeah, it could be."

"Laurel said she and Hart would keep trying to untangle the connections, but she also sort of gave me the go-ahead to try our hand at it. She wants to figure out who did this almost as much as we do."

"So, that's what we'll do," Jack said.

Chapter Fourteen

"So, let's get started," Carlyle said. Even though her head and side throbbed. Even though her eyes felt weirdly prickly. Even though she kind of wanted to crawl into her bed and cry for a hundred years.

But that was a feeling to be avoided, so why not go whole-hog on this? Familiar territory, all in all. Push down the emotional garbage and focus on the danger, on solving the mystery. What else could matter?

"No, you're going to bed, Car."

She was about to argue with Cash—no one got to tell her what to do and so on and so forth, but Walker gave her the subtlest shake of the head. And she had no idea *why* that made her feel something close to ashamed. Like maybe he understood what it felt like...to deal with the garbage rather than the danger. Like, maybe just maybe, that's why he had a wife and a kid on the way.

Because he'd let the garbage go.

She didn't know why everything suddenly felt *different*. Like that unbelievable explosion—ranking pretty damn low on the list of traumatic events on her life—felt like it had detonated something inside of her.

Or maybe it was watching that detective—so sure of her-self, so professional, so kick-butt—be worried about potty stools and be happily married to a husband who looked like he'd move heaven and earth to reverse time and not have her hurt, even though she was in this dangerous job.

Cash helped Carlyle to her feet, and she didn't fight him. She felt like spun glass, and the wrong move would shatter her—like she had in the hospital. If she cried in front of him twice in one day, she was quite certain she would literally die of embarrassment.

So she just let herself be led away, and tried to turn off all the vulnerable parts of her brain. Disassociate. Find some detached place to be.

But she just kept seeing Laurel's husband storming into her hospital room. Walker shaking his head at her. Cash angrily standing in that waiting room demanding to see her.

"I keep thinking you're feeling more yourself, then you get real, real quiet. I know they checked you out, but are you sure you don't have a concussion?"

"Not a concussion." *Just a mental crisis.*

He pulled the instructions he'd taken from her out of his pocket. "It says you can take a shower. Let's do that."

"Together?"

He laughed. "As enticing an offer as that is, *you* are resting tonight. Shower. Are you hungry? I can go hunt you down a snack. Then, *sleep.* Lots of sleep. No staying up late. No getting up early."

"Sure, Dad."

He winced, which *almost* brought her some joy. Not *everything* inside of her had been rearranged today if she could enjoy making him uncomfortable, and that was a relief.

"Go on," he said, not rising to the bait. "Can you handle the shower on your own?" He looked over the paper once more. "Don't wash your hair," he instructed.

She plucked the paper from his hands. "I'll handle it."

He opened his mouth, then shut it. "Okay, you can handle it."

She thought that was going to be that. He'd turn and leave, and she could take her shower in peace and figure out how to shore up all these cracks in her armor. Put all these rearranged pieces of herself back in the right order so that she didn't want to cry. So she didn't want to ask him ridiculous things like *where is this going? Will you ever love me like that detective's husband loves her? Like Walker loves Mary?*

But Cash didn't walk away. He kept *talking*. "But sometimes, you let other people handle it. Because I can't take that scrape on your head away. Or the fact you got *stabbed* to save my daughter. So you could just let me do this. You take a shower, I'll get you some food, and you'll give me a bit of room to fuss over you before you go to sleep."

Fuss. She hated to be fussed over. Wasn't that why she was always saying the shocking thing? When her brothers had gotten all soft over her, it had made her miss her mother so much she thought she wouldn't survive the *weight* of it. "I really don't want to cry in front of you again," she said, because if *anything* made her brothers run, it was that.

Cash, on the other hand, shrugged. Unbothered. "I have a kid. I can handle tears. It's one of my few talents."

It was true. At the hospital he'd just held her. Let her not talk. He'd just…acted like it was a perfectly fine and normal thing to do to cry. He was just doing all this *taking care*, and what had she done for him? What *could* she do?

She sucked at taking care. The only thing she was good at was diving into things headfirst—like this afternoon with the detective, which hadn't gone well at all.

And she'd had to watch the detective's real life. That

man's expression when he looked at his wife. Love and worry and just this perfect picture of *life*.

Like what Mary and Walker were building. Like so many of the people here, and she'd sworn to herself she never wanted all that, but now she was *surrounded* and…and…

God, she had to make this stop. And she knew how. Face it head-on. Freak him out so he bailed. "We need to have the talk."

Cash's eyebrows drew together. "What talk?"

"The talk. The you-and-me talk. The…what-the-hell-are-we-doing talk. Because there's just…all these threads, and we can't keep knotting them."

He studied her like he was afraid she'd suffered the concussion he was so worried about, when she knew her head was just fine. Even if her words weren't. Even if *she* wasn't, at the heart of things.

"I know I'm doing this wrong. Hell, that's how I do things, so why not? You just dive right in."

"Get in the shower. I'll get you something to eat. You'll rest and—"

"I don't want that! I don't want *this*!" She pointed a little erratically at herself because she had no words for what she felt. Only this anxiety-fueled gesture. Only this need to put a stop to all this before…before…before…

She didn't know before *what*. Just *before*.

"Car, I'd love to follow, but I just plain don't."

"I know that. You think I don't know that?" She was off the rails, and she didn't know how to get back on them except to explode everything. "I don't need you to tell me you're in love with me. I just need to know that you could be, eventually. That…eventually… That… It's just… You've been married. Had a kid. I haven't. And I never thought I'd want something so…boring. But I guess, I think, maybe I do. Not like, *today*. Just…someday. So, we should be on the same page about that, because there's too much tangled and rooted here to just…bump up against that someday in the future and need to walk away."

For a moment, he stood there like a statue. An awful statue. Because she couldn't read what he thought of any of that, and so she had the space to think of all the worst-case scenarios she'd just introduced.

Because that's what you do, Carlyle Daniels. Create worst-case scenarios.

But when he spoke, his voice was strangely…raspy. Like each word held such great weight it scraped against his throat.

"Hawk came in and said a civilian had been hurt, and we knew it had to be you. I just…went dark. Hollowed out. I know fear. I've lived with that bastard most of my life, and this was that. The kind you just… It takes over. You are reminded you have *no* control."

She'd been there—more times than she could count. So many times she'd given up on the idea of control a long time ago.

"Your brother asks me about love," he said disgustedly. "Fair enough, I guess, but then my *daughter* asks me. Now you…and I don't know." He raked his fingers through his hair, leaving it unruly. "My track record sucks. My…radar sucks."

She didn't understand where he was going with this, and she wanted to poke and prod more about her brother and Izzy asking him about *love*, but something about his panic eased her own. "*You* don't suck."

He sighed and met her gaze. Not quite so panicked, but she didn't know what had taken over. Something…resigned. "I'm glad you think so. But… You have to understand. A while back, I figured that was it. I made my mistake, was going to pay for it forever, so that was *it*."

Ouch. Well, she hadn't expected it to be that quite cut-and-dried, but now she had to get rid of him so she could cry in peace. "That's all you had to say. We don't have to drag it out." She moved for the bathroom door—because like hell she'd cry again. "We don't have to—"

But he stepped into the bathroom doorway so she couldn't answer, his expression stormy. "Would you shut up and let me finish? You think *you're* panicking? I know how wrong this can go, and I've got a daughter to think about. My panic wins."

"I actually prefer to win," she grumbled, crossing her arms over her chest.

He made a huffing sound, almost like a laugh. But then he got all serious again. "Carlyle, I don't know how to answer all your questions. I'm still…sorting everything out. But let's start with that I am not sitting here thinking… *I could never marry or have kids with this woman.* It's certainly not some…off-the-table thing."

That was not romantic. It really shouldn't be romantic. Was her bar so low? Or was it she just understood how much that must…mess with him. How much *she* must mess with a man who cut off everything he could for so long.

So she nodded. "Well, I guess that's all I was asking."

"Maybe you should ask for a hell of a lot more," he said, looking downright *sad*.

They really were just two messed up, messy people. But she didn't mind that, didn't think it was too terrible. Not when they really wanted to…be good people, help people. Maybe they had a lot of stuff to work through, but they weren't *bad*.

So maybe all this *more* everyone kept talking about

wasn't *more* at all. It was just having the kind of self-aware-
ness to know what she really wanted—outside of what anyone else thought.

"You know, I don't have a kid. I think that makes fear
different. It must. But I've also been pretty well acquainted
with fear most my life. I know far too intimately how tenuous it all is. How little control *anyone* has. So no, I don't
need to ask for *more*, Cash." She moved forward and
wrapped her arms around him and squeezed tight—even
though it sent a bolt of pain through her side. "Not from
you. I think you're physically and psychologically incapa-
ble of giving less than you've got."

He ran a hand down her back. "I hope that's true."

But she didn't hope. She knew.

Just like she knew she couldn't rest. They couldn't rest
until they found something. Because they were all in danger until this mystery got solved.

But for a little while, she'd give him what he asked for.
The space to fuss. And she'd try really hard not to hate it.

CASH FINALLY CONVINCED Carlyle to get into the shower, then
he went to the kitchen and put together some food on a tray
like Mary usually did. It wasn't as nice as when Mary did
it, but it would get the job done.

Fuel. Carlyle needed rest and fuel. And once he made
sure she got those things, he could go figure out this whole
Butch Scott thing. And once he did *that*, maybe they could
figure out the personal stuff.

He had to breathe through the tightness in his chest. A
panic born of…well, failure. Everything with Chessa had
been such a spectacular failure. Here he was twelve years
later, still dealing with it. Even though she was dead. It
wasn't that he thought Carlyle was like that. It was more…

Well, he supposed he couldn't help but blame himself for not finding a way to make things work with Chessa, for not finding a way to get through to her.

Intellectually, he knew better. Love didn't solve addiction. It couldn't erase the marks of an unsteady and abusive childhood. Even if he'd been able to find it within himself to love her, he couldn't change her.

But the guilt stayed. Because he'd wanted a better outcome for Izzy, and for her mother.

So, for the time being, he'd turn his attention to trying to figure out who killed Chessa. Maybe that could ease some of his guilt, and then…then he could really think about what a future with Carlyle looked like.

The future and thinking about it scared the living daylights out of him ever since he'd first dropped Izzy off at kindergarten.

He shook it all away. Focused on the task at hand. That's what had gotten him through for the past few years. One step before the other.

So he took the tray of food to Carlyle's room. She was sitting at the window, looking out at the night sky. That must have been what she'd been doing the night someone had been at Izzy's window. Had that wistful, sad look been on her face then too?

He wanted to find some way to take that wistfulness, that sadness away. She deserved so much more than *this*. But didn't they all? Maybe *deserved* just flat-out didn't matter. Maybe there was only making the best out of what you had.

And the fact she was here. Carlyle being whole and wholly her was a best. A bright spot. "All right. You should eat."

She turned to look at him, then her eyes dropped to the tray. She swallowed, hard. "I thought you'd have Mary put something together."

"She and Izzy had their heads together ordering stuff for the baby. Didn't want to interrupt. Sorry if it's not up to par." He set it on the table within reach of where she was sitting.

She shook her head, her eyes bright. "It's great. I'm... I'm pretty used to doing everything on my own. I guess it's been easy to let Mary swoop in because she's just...her."

"It's what she does."

"Yeah, and it's what you do too, I'm starting to realize." She reached forward, picked up a piece of cheese. "But I also know that means you'll try to tell me to eat, to sleep, and it's not going to happen. You're not doing the work without me. Either we both sleep or we both work. The end. But I think we need to work. I think we need to figure out who this half-brother you didn't know about is."

"I knew about him. Chessa just claimed...less of a familial connection. Which makes sense. Chessa's parents were a bit of a mess. She used to say her father had impregnated half the county. He was an addict himself. Abusive."

"I'm not going to feel sorry for her. Even if she's dead. Anyone who'd sell their daughter doesn't get my sympathy. I don't care if it's the addiction talking."

Cash knew he would always have a complicated relationship with feeling sympathy and grief toward Chessa. But he'd always found some comfort in that his family got to just wholesale hate her, blame her. It was simple for them, and even though he couldn't partake, it felt good it could be simple for someone.

And this felt good in a different way. Because no matter what Izzy thought or worried about, Carlyle was so wholly on her side. Always.

"I'm not asking you to feel sorry for her. I'm just trying to make it clear. She could have half siblings everywhere.

It doesn't necessarily mean Chessa had a relationship with Butch, or knew they were siblings. Even with the same last name."

"But they were. So maybe *he* did, even if she didn't?"

"Maybe. I don't remember meeting him. He was more Anna's age. I think that's why she remembered the name. I'm sure he was trouble like the rest of the Scotts. Nobody really had a chance, growing up like that."

"I imagine Jack is already looking into what kind of trouble he's been in," she said, continuing to eat.

"Yes. Palmer will be doing his own searches too. So there's no reason for you to—"

"From here on out, we're in this together, bud. No more independent work. So, unless you're planning on taking a break, I'm not either."

He sighed. She was pale, and her hair was in a messy knot on her head as she'd followed the instructions and had not washed it. She looked in desperate need of that break. "*I* haven't been stabbed and nearly exploded, Carlyle."

She shook her head, unmoved. "Lucky you. Doesn't change anything."

He sighed. There would be no getting through to her, so he supposed he had to just give in. But not without conditions. "You finish your food. Drink some water. Take something for that headache I know you're pretending you don't have. Once you do all that, we'll join Jack and Palmer downstairs. But not before you take a little care of yourself."

"I always take care of myself," she replied, that typical flash of defiance in her eyes.

He crouched next to her seat so they were eye to eye. "It's not *yourself* anymore, Car. Got it?"

She held his gaze for a very long time. Then she nodded.

And leaned forward and pressed her mouth to his, gently. Cash let the kiss linger, until she pulled away.

"That goes both ways, Cash. You got that?"

"Yeah, I think we both got it."

Chapter Fifteen

When they went down to the living room, there was what Carlyle could only describe as a war room set up. They were treating it like one of their cold cases.

Palmer had joined the fray, sitting in a chair with a laptop in his lap. Zeke was back from picking up the dogs and was conferring with Grant over a bulletin board on wheels they must have rolled out once she'd gone upstairs. Anna rocked Caroline in the corner chair, while telling Grant to add things or take things off the bulletin board. Hawk stood closer to the entryway, speaking into his phone in low tones.

When Zeke spotted Carlyle enter the room, he scowled. "You should rest."

"There's no point. I'm not going to sleep knowing you all are down here working this out." She walked over to the bulletin board, ignoring the way Zeke's glare was now aimed at Cash.

Honestly. *Men.*

"What have you all come up with in the past hour?"

Jack was the one who took the reins first. "It's looking more and more like Ferguson was the body in the building. We'll need dental records to confirm, but no one's seen him, and everything Bent County would release to Brink leans toward Ferguson."

"No whereabouts on Chessa's half-brother?" Carlyle asked.

Jack shook his head. "They're looking, thanks to Detective Delaney-Carson. But he likely knows he's being looked for, so that'll make it more difficult."

Carlyle stared at all the seemingly disparate events on the bulletin board. "What's the endgame here? We have a failed kidnapping, a murder—probably two—and an explosion. What is the goal?"

"Maybe there isn't one," Anna replied, considering. "Just destruction? Pain? They wanted to frame Cash, like Izzy said. So maybe that's it?"

But they were doing a really bad job of framing Cash, Carlyle thought to herself, frowning at the bulletin board as she tried to find a thread that made any sense. Maybe they couldn't have predicted her as an alibi for Chessa's murder, but they had to know he'd have one for the explosion. Unless there was something about that which would point to Cash?

"Some guy messes with *my* sister, I'm going to mess him up." Zeke looked over at Cash pointedly.

"I hardly *messed* with Chessa," Cash said darkly. "Quite the opposite."

"It wouldn't have to be true. Could have just been how Chessa framed things to her brother."

Carlyle rolled her eyes. "But Cash didn't think she had much of a relationship with this Butch. Chessa claimed him as a cousin when they were together. It's possible they didn't even know or care they were related. Just because they had the same father named on their birth certificate doesn't mean much—as you and I both know." After all, the name of the father on her birth certificate had not been accurate.

"Maybe something changed in the past few years," Grant

suggested. "Maybe they didn't know about each other a decade ago or didn't care. But something brought them together more recently and they figured the connection out?" Grant pointed at a paper tacked to the bulletin board. "Butch Scott has had trouble with the law since he was a minor. As an adult, a lot of the charges deal with drugs. Could be they started to run in the same circles."

"Then how does Bryan Ferguson get messed up in this?" Jack said. He'd apparently at least accepted his employee was part of it, but Carlyle got the feeling Jack didn't believe in Ferguson having full-on involvement. Maybe because he'd likely ended up dead.

Maybe Jack was right, to an extent. He knew Ferguson. Had worked with him. Been his boss. Jack was hardly the type to believe in someone who didn't prove they were trustworthy. Carlyle wasn't even sure he trusted *her*.

"Whether intentionally or not, we know Ferguson helped Tripp get Chessa out of jail on bond that night last year. Or at least kept it from Jack for as long as possible," Cash said. "Whether it was true or not, Chessa said Tripp was her boyfriend at the time. Chessa escapes, Tripp dies. But Chessa doesn't just escape, she disappears. She lies very low for a *year.*"

"And that was abnormal?" Carlyle asked Cash, but it was Anna who answered.

"She never went more than a few months without demanding money from somebody around here."

"Did you all pay her off?"

"At first," Cash said, clearly unhappy that he had. "But once the drug addiction became evident, we cut it off. She never stopped asking though. Until this all happened. I figured she was just...finally aware enough that she'd crossed that final line. She'd engaged in actively harming one of us, talked too freely of getting her hands on Izzy. I thought maybe she'd figured out nothing good was going to come from messing with us."

Carlyle shook her head. She was no addict expert, but she understood patterns. "If she stayed away that long, she had access to money to buy drugs, or just access to the drugs themselves. That pattern doesn't stop because someone finally becomes self-aware. Especially someone who paints themselves a victim. She didn't realize anything. She found a steady mark."

"Butch Scott?" Anna suggested.

"Maybe."

"Well, we can't do anything with that information until the cops find him. And you're not going off in the middle of the night to search, so I guess it's bedtime."

Carlyle didn't even bother to acknowledge Zeke had spoken. She was studying Butch's rap sheet. She tapped the end of it. "He's also kept his nose clean for the past year almost. After *years* of not going more than four months without getting some kind of arrest." She looked at Jack. "We want to find out where he is, sure. But we also want to know where they *were*. Them both going quiet makes me think they were together."

"Together not getting into trouble?" Grant asked dubiously.

Carlyle shook her head and looked at Zeke. Because she knew he had to be thinking the same thing she was. "Sure, you can stay out of trouble by not finding any, but that's not their MO. So the other option is they found someone to *hide* their trouble. Someone—or *someones*—who could hide it *for* them."

"You're suggesting Ferguson kept them from getting

in trouble," Jack said, and though his voice was detached, even Carlyle could tell this was eating at him.

As much as Carlyle wanted to go easy on him, because she was that softy Cash had accused her of being and didn't want to hurt Jack worse than he was hurting himself, they had to follow the truth to find the truth. "He knew the ins and outs of Sunrise Sheriff's Department, didn't he? And likely Bent County too."

Jack didn't reply, but that was reply enough.

"You guys searched his apartment when you looked for him?"

"Bent County did," Jack said. "They're making sure Sunrise is staying as far away from this as possible."

Carlyle nodded, thinking. "What about other property he owned? Or Tripp Anthony? Just because he's dead doesn't mean he doesn't connect to the big picture here."

"Tripp lived on our property, in the cabin Walker stayed at when he first came here. Before that, he lived at home with his parents in Hardy," Anna said. "They would have been the ones in charge of everything when he died. And he's been dead this whole time."

"Still, it wouldn't hurt to look into what he had. Into *his* known associates, as well as Bryan's. Find those little connections that might lead to bigger ones. The cops are going to do what they can, and I know Laurel wants to get to the truth of this, but she's been hurt."

"So, we pick up the slack," Zeke said.

Carlyle nodded, turning her attention to Jack. "You know how they'll go about it. How they'll approach these connections. We need to do it differently. So we're not just treading the same water. Where are they going to look first?"

Jack was quiet for a moment, but eventually seemed to relent. "They'll focus on Butch. How he relates to the case, to Chessa—only to Ferguson if and when he's identified as the dead man. But right now? They're going to focus on finding Butch and getting info about him."

Carlyle nodded, because she'd figured as much. "Okay, so let's focus on Ferguson. And Tripp, to an extent. Let them focus on the Butch angle, we'll focus on this one."

"I'll text Brink to look into any property Ferguson *and* Tripp might have had access to," Jack said. "Maybe it leads us to something before this started, but it won't stop anything. Ferguson being dead means whoever killed him will know we'll look into him. They won't be anywhere that ties them to him."

"If they're smart," Carlyle agreed. She studied the bulletin board, because so many things didn't add up. It was possible everyone was just so clever that even the Bent County detectives and this group of trained investigators couldn't see their pattern, but Carlyle was beginning to wonder if it didn't make any sense because it was scattershot. Because there was no *solid* goal.

She glanced at Cash.

Except maybe…revenge.

CASH BOWED OUT of the discussions a little early to go put Izzy to bed. He wasn't surprised exactly that Carlyle had decided to come with him. He'd thought the case and wanting to crack it would come first, but she walked away without a backward glance.

For her, Izzy was a priority too. And that mattered a great deal.

"She's going to ask about the bandage," he said to Carlyle. It was his first instinct to hide it, or lie to Izzy about it, but as much as Izzy was *his* daughter to care for and protect, it was Carlyle's injury, because she'd gotten messed up in his life. Maybe it was her call on this one.

"She didn't know I was at the hospital?"

"I doubt Mary told her or she would have insisted on seeing you a lot earlier. They've been so happily busy with baby stuff, I didn't want to interrupt."

Cash didn't know why that made Carlyle frown, but he didn't have a chance to ask because they'd reached Mary's open door.

Not only were Mary and Izzy sitting next to each other, heads practically touching as they looked at something on Mary's laptop, but Walker was sitting in the armchair in the corner flipping through a pregnancy book. Copper was curled in the corner, but he lifted his head when Cash and Carlyle stepped in the room. Walker eyed Carlyle though didn't say anything.

"Time for bed, Iz," Cash said.

Izzy rolled her eyes, but she got up at the same time. "It's summer. Why can't I stay up late?"

"It's late enough. And you've got chores in the morning, just like the rest of us."

She groaned, but before she left the room, she turned back to Mary. "*I* like the name Levi."

"We are not naming our kid after some boy band singer," Walker said from his spot in the corner. Clearly this little argument had been going on for a while now.

"He plays the *drums*, Uncle Walker," Izzy said with the kind of contempt only a twelve-year-old girl can muster. Walker hid a smile.

"Oh, Levi Jones?" Carlyle said, perking up. "He's *hot*."

Izzy nodded emphatically and Cash couldn't stop himself from pulling a face, but Carlyle grinned at him, and it was nice to see these parts of her back. The clearheaded investigator she'd been downstairs. The mischievous woman who liked to tease.

He liked the softer sides of her too, hoped she'd get more used to those coming out, but he knew she was *feeling* her best when she could cause a little discomfort. He had no idea why he found that so damn attractive.

They got Izzy through her bedtime routine, and Cash tucked her in while Carlyle waited outside the door.

"How come she has a bandage on her head?" Izzy asked, surprising Cash that she'd noticed and hadn't said anything to Carlyle. He'd been ready to let Carlyle take the lead on this, but Izzy was asking out of earshot.

"She just had a little accident when she went to help the detective." Which was mostly true. "She's good. I promise." And that was the important part. She was good.

Izzy nodded, but she was chewing on her lip. Clearly still worried. Cash brushed some hair off her forehead. He couldn't promise everything would be fine like he wanted to. "We're getting to the bottom of everything. One step at a time. We'll get there." He kissed her forehead, then moved to leave the room, Copper settled into his dog bed under the window.

But Izzy spoke before he'd made it to the door.

"You know, if you and Carlyle got married and had a baby, that'd be okay."

He froze. Inside and out. What the hell was he supposed to say to *that*? Except maybe no more days with Mary baby planning.

Cash had to clear his throat to speak as he turned to look at her, but he couldn't see her expression in the dark. "Ah, well, it's a bit...soon for all that, Iz."

"That's okay. But I like babies, so..."

"I... Okay," he agreed, because he didn't know what else

to do. Because that was *quite* the one-eighty from earlier. Because this whole Carlyle thing wasn't even a *week* old, and everyone was already throwing all this at him. "Night, Izzy. I love you."

This was why people didn't live with their families into adulthood.

He stepped into the hallway, closing the door behind him.

Carlyle studied him. "Looking a little pale," she said, as if concerned, but he saw the amusement in her eyes.

"You heard her, didn't you?"

She laughed, hooked her arm with his and leaned into him as they walked down the hallway to his room. "Yeah. Don't worry, I'm sure I went a little pale too. I do not know that *I* like babies. Particularly coming out of me."

Cash only grunted. They walked into his bedroom, still arm in arm, but once inside his room, he pulled his arm away from her. He pointed at her.

"Now, no funny business."

She grinned, sliding her arms around his waist. "Aw, come on. Just a little." That grin stayed in place, and he saw a kind of relaxed happy that hadn't been in her eyes all day. Understandably. But there were shadows under her eyes and that bandage on her head.

"You need your rest." But he dropped his mouth to hers, because good in the midst of bad was starting to become... not the distraction he always feared, but a foundation to get through the bad.

Still, he bundled her into his bed, and it didn't take much for her to fall asleep. She was exhausted and injured. He was a little exhausted himself apparently, because the next thing he knew he woke with a start, not quite sure what it was that had woken him up. Carlyle was curled up next to him and as he lay there and listened to the sounds of the house in the dark, he didn't hear a thing. He glanced at the clock. Four in the morning.

Early yet, even before Mary's usual ungodly wake-up call, but Cash knew he had lots to do today, and there was no point trying to get another hour's sleep when he'd likely lay there and make too many mental to-do lists to count. Might as well get up and start the *do* portion of his day.

Palmer and Zeke had handled the dogs last night, but the truck would need cleaning out. There was paperwork to do from yesterday's events with the dogs—he'd have to have Carlyle write up a report for what had happened. Much as he didn't want her to have to relive the explosion part, it was important to keep records of everything the dogs did outside the ranch.

He slid out of bed, being careful not to wake Carlyle. She stirred a little, but rolled over and was quickly breathing evenly again. Swiftie stayed put on her side of the bed. He grabbed his clothes, his phone, then carefully eased out of the room.

Clearly, everyone in the house was still asleep, which was good. Often, in the middle of danger or investigations there was always someone up and about, putting too much time and worry into it. But everyone upstairs was paired off now, and there were kids and kids-to-be in the house besides Izzy. Life—real life—was starting to take over all the ways they'd isolated themselves since their parents had died.

Except for maybe Jack, who very well could be awake in his room working on something, but Cash hoped he was asleep.

It was dark and still as he walked downstairs. Not even the telltale sound of a baby crying or a rocking chair creaking. He decided to forgo coffee. He didn't want to chance waking anyone up, particularly when a lot of them had likely been up too late looking into Bryan Ferguson.

Cash disengaged the security system so he could step outside into the cool, dark morning. On a normal morning, he would have left it off, knowing people would be coming and going for the rest of the day, but it was early and dark enough he thought it best to reengage the system once he was out. The cameras always ran no matter what, but the alarms were usually only in place overnight.

Once that was taken care of, he turned and looked out into the dark night around the ranch. He lifted his face to the sky. The moon was a tiny sliver above his cabin in the distance, clear and bright despite its diminished size. The sky sparkled and pulsed. And for a moment, Cash just stood there and absorbed this odd time of night, this quiet.

Home. This had always been his home. Through good times and very bad times, Hudson Ranch had been the roots that had kept him tethered. Izzy had come along and only sunk those roots deeper—but he'd only been able to do that for her because of his family and this place.

He didn't let himself wallow in self-pity as a rule. It always felt too close to going down Chessa's line of thinking about the world, but Cash realized he'd gotten very bad about counting his blessings. He had shrunk his world down to Izzy and just Izzy. He *knew* he'd been lucky in the face of tragedy, but he hadn't *felt* it in a long time.

Even with the danger going on around them, he felt that gratitude in this moment. He'd had this place, this foundation to keep Izzy safe all these years. And he could manage all the years to come.

A streak of a shooting star flashed across the sky. Like a good omen.

He was ready for a few good omens. He'd been white-knuckling it for so long, and there was a part of his brain telling him to keep at it. There were murders and explosions. Now was not the time to *relax and enjoy.*

But for all the *wrong*, there was good. His daughter. His family. His dogs and business. And the surprising detour that was Carlyle Daniels. A good reminder of what he'd realized himself last night. No matter the bad, the foundation of good was how you muddled through.

Between Bent County, the Sunrise Sheriff's Department, his family and the Daniels siblings, they would get to the bottom of this. He'd long ago stopped depending on answers for a great many things—when your parents disappeared into thin air never to be heard from again, that was the life lesson.

But today, he was going to believe they'd find this problem's answers. He'd give Izzy the answers about her mother's death that he'd never been able to find about his own. No matter what it took.

He set out across the yard, heading for the dog barns. He'd get his chores done early, then move into investigation mode. They could afford a full break from training for a day or two, as long as the dogs got exercise.

So focused on this plan of action, he almost didn't stop his forward progress even as his gaze went over the dark shadow of his cabin. But a few steps beyond the cabin, the image of it, the wrongness of *something*, caught up with him.

He paused, frowned, then turned back toward it. He'd seen…something. Probably just the reflection of the moon. But could they be too careful right now?

He retraced his steps silently. He studied the shadowy cabin. Everything was barely visible in the dim light of the moon and stars. It was all dark now. No light. No flash of anything. Definitely just a random reflection, he told himself. Mentally urging himself to move on.

But his body didn't listen. It was rooted to the spot as he squinted through the dark at the cabin. He didn't see anything this time, but...he *heard* something. A rustle, an exhale. *Something.*

He should go back to the house and get a gun. He should text one of his brothers. There were a lot of things he should do, but the closer he got to the cabin, the more he could discern that the noise was a voice. Someone was inside the cabin. *Talking.* He couldn't make out words, but a window or door must have been open because he could hear the tone and tenor of the voice.

Normally, that would have sent him back to the house immediately. Normally, he would have made all the right choices in this moment.

But the voice clearly said, "You have to." In a voice he *recognized.*

It wasn't possible. It couldn't be possible.

But he *knew* that voice.

So he moved toward the cabin, rather than away like he should.

Chapter Sixteen

Once Cash reached the porch, he could tell the front door was cracked open. It was too dark to determine if it had been forced or not, but it didn't matter when he knew that voice. It was clearly coming from inside, and they were either talking to themselves or their audience was completely silent.

Cash crept up the stairs, listening to every word that was spoken. It couldn't be possible, but...

"I told you it was a bad idea." There was a beat, the speaker clearly listening.

Then it dawned on him. She was on the phone. Had the flash of light he'd seen been a phone screen?

"You're the one who had to do the explosion," she said, her voice getting louder in frustration. A frustration he was so well acquainted with.

Was this some dream? A break with reality? Everyone had said she was dead. *Dead.* People he trusted. People he loved. Everyone certain she was murdered. There were cops who thought *he* was a suspect.

But that was Chessa's voice. He knew Chessa's voice. Maybe they hadn't spent much time together in the past few years, but her voice had haunted him for years. He had listened and watched for her vigilantly for so long now, it was hard to believe he'd be wrong. He couldn't imagine anyone sounding this much like her and not *being* her. Or talking about explosions—the one that was clearly connected to his current predicament.

Cash crept closer to the door. Maybe if he could get some glimpse at the person talking, he could convince himself there was no possible way—

But the door swung open, and he had to jump back to avoid being smacked in the face by it.

The woman who stepped out into the night was… It was Chessa. Maybe it was dark, but the moon and stars offered *some* light. Maybe someone out there looked *a lot* like her in the shadows. But he knew this woman, and even in the dark he just knew it was…her. Short and slightly built. That I'll-mess-anyone-up posture he'd once found attractive, when he'd wanted to see *everyone* messed up.

Chessa wasn't dead. No matter what anyone had said. She was *here*.

"We've got company," she said into the phone at her ear. She didn't seem surprised to see him. Just sort of grim about it. She shoved the phone in her pocket. "Where's your posse?" she asked dismissively, the shadow of her chin jerking toward the house.

Just like always. Such a *Chessa* movement and statement. It was *her*.

Cash couldn't get over the pure shock of it all. Even now. Standing here, staring at her. It was real and he didn't know how to process it.

He didn't think she was high. He'd spent that first year of Izzy's life learning the signs in Chessa. There was a *movement* to her when she was high. Tonight she seemed still, controlled and stone-cold sober. That was honestly more of a concern than her being alive. High Chessa was volatile and dangerous, but Sober Chessa used all that rage and trauma to cause true, focused damage.

"You're alive," he managed to say, no matter how pointless that sounded in the quiet night around them. "How the hell did you convince people you were dead?"

She made a noise, not quite a laugh, but sort of amused. "I can't believe that worked. Pays to have friends on the inside."

"Ferguson?"

She didn't act surprised he knew. "Poor guy. All *riddled* with guilt with pulling one over on his little cop buddies. He was going to break. Had to take care of it." She sighed like she was upset over a broken nail. "Oh well. He did what we needed."

"Who's *we*?"

"Wouldn't you like to know?" She shook her head. "You really thought you'd ever be rid of me, baby?"

Sometimes, it made his skin crawl that she was Izzy's mother, but this was beyond all of those old guilts and frustrations. She had somehow convinced an entire law enforcement agency she was dead. But she wasn't, and she was *here*, sneaking around the ranch.

"What are you doing here, Chessa?" he asked, doing his best to sound bored instead of enraged.

"What do you think? I'm going to get my hands on her. I'll never stop trying. *Never.*" She moved forward, but Cash didn't see any kind of weapon on her. She just poked her finger into his chest.

He would never understand. She hadn't wanted to be a mother, hadn't wanted to stick around. She'd *left*, and he hadn't made that hard on her so he couldn't ever understand this need to keep popping back up. To keep trying to *hurt* the daughter she didn't want.

Because she was a damn wound every day of his life. And Izzy's.

But her poke turned into a shove, almost like she couldn't quite stop herself, and he was still reeling from her being *alive* that it landed hard enough that he stumbled back.

"I'm going to take her," Chessa said, giving him another push, though he was ready for it this time. He held his ground.

"Why do you think it's going to go differently this time?" And it made him uneasy, because she might not be the most rational person on the planet—high or sober—but Izzy was just as protected as she always was, and Chessa had never once succeeded at getting her hands on their daughter.

Chessa didn't respond to his question. Instead, she lunged at him. A terrible attempt at a tackle, but then she kicked his shin, and he went down just enough that she jumped on top of him.

It was all so...surreally ridiculous. Cash wasn't quite sure how to proceed, except to protect himself from her weak attempts at punching and kicking. She was short and never'd had much meat on her bones, but she seemed nothing but skin and bones now.

He had the height and the weight to easily stop her blows. He couldn't fathom why she was trying to fight him when he had the physical upper hand. He rolled over on top of her, pinning her hands above her head. She stopped moving, but he could see the way she grinned up at him in the breaking light of dawn.

"You won't hit me, Cash. All that noble Hudson blood. You won't do anything except sit there and take it." She lifted her leg, clearly trying to land a knee, and failing as she tried to free her arms from his grasp. "I'm your daughter's mother. You wouldn't do *anything* to hurt me."

"That's where you're wrong, Chessa. Because I'd do anything and hurt any damn person to protect my daughter."

"I'm counting on it," Chessa said, then she smiled up at him and it was clue enough for what was coming. But he wasn't quite fast enough. The blow hit him from behind, from someone much bigger than him. It didn't knock him out, though it hurt like the devil, but it did knock him off Chessa.

And before he could get to his feet, she rolled over and jabbed something sharp and painful into his thigh.

And then everything went black.

CARLYLE COULDN'T BELIEVE how long she'd slept, or that she'd slept through Cash leaving the room. She was usually a light sleeper, but she supposed the past few days had really taken it out of her.

She sat up in Cash's bed, then yawned and stretched as she blinked at the bright sun streaming through the windows. Her body hurt. All over. She lifted her shirt to peek at her stitches.

She frowned a little. They'd bled through the bandage she'd slapped on last night after she'd showered. Maybe she should have mentioned something at the hospital the other day, but she had just wanted to get out of there.

And she definitely didn't want to go *back*. So, she'd just slap another bandage on and hope the problem went away. Because there was too much to do today. Way too much.

And Cash had let her sleep the entire morning away. She was going to have to have a talking to with that man. She didn't mind being taken care of *a little*, but not when so many important things were going on. Hopefully, there'd been some kind of break in the case.

If there wasn't, well, she was damn well going to find one.

She slid out of bed with a wince. Her head wasn't too bad, but man, her side was really killing her. She'd need to take something for the pain when she changed the bandage. All of her supplies were down in her room, so that'd be the first stop.

She let Swiftie out. "Have you been up here the whole time?" she asked, giving the dog a pat on the head as she walked out into the hallway.

But she stopped abruptly. Izzy was coming out of her own room down the hallway. She came to the same abrupt halt.

A deep, awkward silence ensued as Izzy studied Carlyle, then the door behind her. Swiftie trotted past Izzy to head downstairs, likely to be let out.

Carlyle didn't know how to sit in an awkward silence, so she cleared her throat. "Uh, you sleep in too?"

"No. I was just up here to get Caroline her doggy," Izzy said, holding up the stuffed animal.

"Your dad isn't…in there," Carlyle said. God knew why. She might love this little girl, but she hardly owed her an *explanation*. She definitely wasn't going to tell a twelve-year-old everything had been perfectly hands-off. Last night at least.

Izzy frowned. "He isn't? I haven't seen him all morning."

"I'm sure he's just…out doing chores." It was the only explanation, but it was strange Izzy hadn't seen him at *all*. He usually made a point of eating breakfast with her. "Did you text him?"

Izzy shook her head. "We all thought he was sleeping in, so we were leaving him to it."

Because they'd likely known *she* was in the room, allegedly with him. The whole family, no doubt. *We all*. Oh, Carlyle wasn't ready to think about *we all*. She knew they all *thought* things, and that was easy to brazen through when it wasn't *true*. But it was true now and…

She blew out a breath. Well, she was going to have to deal with it, wasn't she? *She'd* been the one to bring up all that future junk. She could hardly get a little gun-shy now that they had an audience.

Carlyle pulled her phone out of her pocket. She sent Cash a quick *where are you* text, then forced herself to smile reassuringly at Izzy. "I bet he's out with the dogs. I just have to grab a few things then I'll go look for him if he doesn't answer."

Izzy chewed on her bottom lip, but she nodded. They headed downstairs and Izzy trailed after her to her bedroom. Carlyle didn't want Izzy to worry, so she decided to forgo the bandage and the painkillers and just grab her work boots and a hat to hide the bump and bandage on her head.

"Have you eaten break—" But before she could shoo Izzy out of the bedroom and to the kitchen, Izzy practically leapt forward.

"Carlyle! You've got blood on your shirt."

Carlyle looked down at her side. Damn stitches. "Oh, that's nothing."

"That's where you had your stitches," Izzy said, frowning so deeply a line formed on her forehead. "Carlyle, you need to go to the doctor!"

Carlyle shook her head. "Nah. I'm good. I just need to change the bandage. No worries. I'll just…"

Izzy took her hand and pulled her into the little half bath room attached to her room. She grabbed a washcloth and ran the hot water. "It could be infected," she said, sounding very adult. Her expression was very stern. Carlyle could certainly physically move past the girl, but she found herself standing in the bathroom, feeling like a child herself.

"It's fine."

Izzy sighed very heavily. "Lift your shirt," she instructed.

Carlyle wasn't much for taking orders, but coming from a *child* she really didn't know how to be a jerk in response, so she did as she was told.

Izzy tutted over the bloody bandage, carefully removed it and threw it in the trash. She gently washed away the blood, sighed over the broken stitches, then applied a new bandage over the gash with adept hands. She had Mary's cool, collected nature about her, and the calm, authoritarian voice Cash used with the dogs.

"You really should go to the doctor if that's not better by tomorrow." She looked up at Carlyle very sternly.

Carlyle could only smile and brush a hand over Izzy's flyaway hair. No wonder she was crazy about her. "You're something, kid."

Izzy's mouth curved a little. "I could be an EMT when I grow up. Help people in emergencies. Sometimes I help the vet when he comes out, but that just makes me sad. The animals don't know what you're saying to them, but people know you're trying to help them. So, I think I'll do that. I'd be good at it."

"Bet your ass you would." Carlyle had no problem seeing her do just that.

This caused Izzy to give her a full-blown smile. But it died quickly. "What if my dad is having an emergency? What if—"

"He has his phone. His dogs. And his brain. I can't promise you he's not… Let's just focus on finding him, and we'll go from there. But no matter what, he's going to be okay." Which she also couldn't promise, but she needed it to be true for herself just as much for Izzy. He had to be fine. He *would* be fine. He was Cash.

Izzy nodded and they walked toward the kitchen. Carlyle slid her arm around Izzy's shoulders, gave them a reassuring squeeze. Again, the move was as much for the girl as it was for herself.

Mary was sitting at the kitchen table with Walker. They both looked up at their entrance, but then Mary frowned. "Where's Cash?"

"He was up early. Really early. I haven't seen him since. Are we sure no one's seen him out and about this morning?"

Mary blinked once, then smiled over at Izzy. "Caroline probably wants that, honey," she said, pointing to the stuffed animal still in Izzy's hand.

"I'll get it to her in a second. So *no one* knows where Dad is?" she demanded, looking at Carlyle, then back at Mary and Walker.

"I'm sure he's out doing chores," Carlyle managed to say, but he hadn't texted her back. So she was getting less and less sure. Still, where would he have gone? People didn't just…disappear.

She thought of the Hudson parents and had to swallow the lump of fear that lodged in her throat.

"He didn't get coffee this morning," Mary said quietly, pointing to the carafe. "His mugs—kitchen and travel—are still right there." She looked over to Walker, who nodded.

"I'll grab Palmer to look at the security footage. Grant and I will go find him," Walker said, making it sound easy. Light and casual as he got to his feet. "Probably hip-deep in dogs somewhere," he said, and flashed Izzy a grin. He gave his wife a quick squeeze on the way out.

Mary nodded. Her expression was calm, but she wrung her hands together in a sign of nerves as Walker strode out of the kitchen.

"The uncles will take care of it," Izzy said, sounding

so calm and collected just like her aunt, but Carlyle saw the terror in her eyes, so she didn't argue. She took Izzy's hand in hers.

"Yeah, besides, if he's with the dogs, we all know he's fine. Those dogs are fierce."

Izzy swallowed and nodded, but her gaze was worried and she stared at the back door. If he'd left, it would be on the security footage. If he was out there on the ranch, Walker and Grant would find him.

If he was in trouble… Well, the Hudsons and the Daniels would come together to get him out of it.

No matter what.

Chapter Seventeen

Cash came to in the dark. His head pounded. His stomach threatened to heave out its contents. He felt fuzzy headed and a little drunk. But he hadn't been drinking. He'd been…

He tried to cast back and remember. Tried to lift a hand, but he couldn't move at all.

He was tied up. To a chair. He looked around, even as his vision seemed to swim. Inside his cabin. That was good, even if nothing else was. Like the roiling nausea in his gut, the complete immobility. None of that was *good*, but he was in his own kitchen, which meant help was not that far away.

He took a breath, trying to steady himself. Bad but not terrible. He could work with this. He would have to.

"This might just be the *best* day," Chessa said.

He turned his head toward her voice. She was smiling at him. Her eyes were bright now, her movements jerky. How he'd gotten in this predicament was a little fuzzy, but he remembered her. Alive. She'd been sober before, but now it was clear she'd taken a hit of something.

Behind her, rifling through his kitchen pantry was a big man.

"Butch, right?" Cash managed. His mouth was dry and trying to speak caused a coughing fit he immediately regretted.

The man didn't respond. Not to him. Not to Chessa. He just opened a jar of peanut butter and gave it a little sniff. As if satisfied by the smell, her re-capped the jar and tossed it into a bag on the ground. While Chessa moved around the kitchen, not doing anything. Just moving.

"I'm getting tired of waiting for him," she said, clearly aiming those words at Butch. That guy had to be Butch. Even though Cash had known of him, maybe seen him a few times, he had no clear recollection of what her cousin or half brother or whatever he was looked like, but they had to be in this together.

"You're always tired of waiting," Butch grumbled. "And it never got you anywhere, so why don't you shut up and let me handle it?"

She scowled at the man's back. Cash watched as her eyes darted toward the knife block on the counter, then back at the man. But she didn't make a move to grab the knives. She just turned to face Cash once more.

She sauntered over to him, got her face real close to his. "Maybe you'd like another hit?" she said, smirking. "A little lighter this time, so you don't pass full out. You never were one for the hard stuff, were you?"

He remembered now. The pain in his leg. She'd shot him up with something. "You were bad choice enough," he managed to say.

She reared back and slapped him across the face. It stung, and made the other side of his head throb, but the blow was hardly terrible and did little. He raised a condescending eyebrow at her.

"Feel big and important?" he asked her, working to keep his voice calm in the face of her increasing agitation so he didn't start coughing again.

She was clearly going to hit him again, but Butch grabbed her arm before she could swing. "Knock it off."

Chessa tried to wrestle her arm away from Butch, but he held firm. "I warned you." His voice was stone-cold. "You start acting this way, you won't get another hit. You'll end up as dead as everyone thinks you are."

Cash was very familiar with the look of seething hate on Chessa's face, but she stopped struggling. "How much longer?" she demanded of Butch through clenched teeth.

"Long as it takes. That's how we stay out of jail, remember?"

She groaned and jerked her arm out of Butch's grasp, but she didn't say anything more, or do anything. Just stood in the corner of the kitchen, and when she couldn't stand that, simply began to pace. She complained, but quietly and under her breath.

Cash kept his gaze on her as he surreptitiously pulled at the cord that tied his arms and legs to the chair. Tied tight with almost no wiggle room. Likely Butch's doing. He was definitely the one in charge and worked with a clearer head and less explosive anger than Chessa.

Which might keep Cash alive longer, but it definitely meant he had less of a chance of escaping. He knew what buttons to push when it came to Chessa. Less so of Butch.

"So, who are we waiting on? You've killed Bryan Ferguson, and I'm sure you're aware the police figured out that you all connect."

Butch didn't react, but Chessa kind of jerked at that, then whirled around so her back was to Cash. Butch went back to his pantry perusal and didn't say anything.

"They also know this is bigger than Bryan. It connects back to Tripp."

This time Butch paused what he was doing and looked

over his shoulder at Cash. "Please, keep talking." He smirked. "The more information, the better."

Cash didn't scowl, though he wanted to. "It's just not going to be rocket science to figure out the connection. Especially once they get ahold of your stepmother."

"Good luck there," Chessa said with a snort, earning her a glare from Butch.

Cash filed that away. Whatever Butch didn't want Chessa going on about was important. Information that could help. Once he got out of here.

Because he *would* get out of here. This was his house, his land and everyone who loved him was within arm's reach.

"This can't end well for you guys," Cash said.

"Don't worry about our plans, honey. We're going to be just fine. You, on the other hand? We're going to—"

"Shut up, Chessa. I'm warning you," Butch said, tossing a box of crackers into his pack. "Not another word."

"You think she's going to be quiet?" Cash said, forcing himself to laugh. If there was one thing he had on his side, it was the certainty that Chessa had a short fuse. "She can't control herself when it comes to anything."

Butch made a little noise, kind of like a laugh himself. "Women," he muttered.

"You've spent twelve years trying to beat me, Chess. You've never won."

"I've won. I'll *win*! Once I make this trade—"

"Hey!" Butch yelled, the volume of it hopefully traveling outside. *Please someone be outside.* "I told you to shut the hell up."

But Chessa was on a roll. Because high or not, controlling her anger had never been in her skill set. She moved toward him, hands in fists.

"You paint yourselves the heroes, but people hate you.

They're going to be so happy to think you're a bad guy. Just look at your parents. Someone hated them so much, they got rid of them without a trace."

"I said that's enough," Butch said angrily. He walked right over to Chessa. Cash braced himself for the blow he thought was coming to her, but it was worse. Butch put his hands around her throat. "You can't shut up. I'll make sure you never talk again." Then he clearly squeezed because Chessa started clawing at his arms and struggling. Her face started to turn purple as Butch choked her.

Cash couldn't just…watch her be killed. No matter what she'd done, who she'd been, this wasn't right. He tried to jerk his body enough to move the chair, to do anything. "Hey! Knock it off!"

Butch didn't pay him any mind. Cash looked around the kitchen, desperately hoping for some inspiration in how to get out of this, how to stop Butch, how to…

Then he saw the phone on the counter kind of shake. He couldn't hear it vibrating over Chessa's gurgles, but any sort of distraction would help.

"Hey! Isn't that your phone ringing?"

Butch looked over at the counter and sighed. He let go of Chessa and she dropped to the ground, gasping for air and pawing at her neck. Alive. Somehow, still alive.

Cash didn't feel relief, exactly. But he pushed all feeling away. He had to focus. Butch had answered the phone, but he didn't say anything besides *yes* or *no*.

Cash pulled at the bonds again. Tight. Too tight. He couldn't really move the chair. The only way he was going to get out of this was to wait it out. To somehow survive until…

Hell, he didn't know. But he wasn't about to give up.

"It's time," Butch said to Chessa. "But if you don't watch

your step, we're leaving the girl behind and maybe your corpse. No trade."

Chessa sneered at Butch, but she got to her feet on shaky legs. "Whatever," she muttered, her voice raspy.

The girl. Why did it always come back to Izzy? "How the hell do you think you're going to get your hands on Izzy? I'm *missing.* You think my family is just going to… what? Leave her home alone? Leave her unprotected? She's got an *army* keeping her safe. You'll never get your hands on her." He said it because it was true, and because it was a reminder to himself. No one was going to let Izzy get hurt.

"We have our ways." Then Chessa pulled out her phone and held it up, like she was taking a picture of him. "Smile, honey. We're about to send your family on a very wild goose chase."

WALKER AND GRANT walked into the kitchen a little while later, and they didn't need to speak for Carlyle to know they hadn't found Cash. Palmer was still looking through security footage, she assumed.

And Cash hadn't texted her back.

But she'd sat at the table and forced herself to eat, if only to keep Izzy company. Anna and Caroline had joined them in the kitchen, pretending not to be worried, but Anna's gaze kept tracking out the window.

Grant's gaze skirted over Izzy, but Walker dove right in. "There's no evidence he ever let the dogs out this morning."

"But he had to. He always does," Izzy said, grabbing onto Carlyle's arm.

"I'm going to go get Palmer," Anna muttered. She passed off Caroline to Mary and left the kitchen.

Izzy leaned into Carlyle and Carlyle held her tight, trying not to let her mind zoom ahead. One step at a time. If he hadn't let the dogs out, something had stopped him. It would be on the security footage. Palmer would have found something, and they'd know how to proceed.

But before Palmer came in or Anna returned, Jack strode in through the back door in his Sunrise SD polo. "Anything?" he demanded.

Mary shook her head. "No."

Jack didn't say anything to that, and Carlyle couldn't read his expression. She supposed Jack, more than any of them, had the most practice keeping a blank expression in the face of potential trauma.

There had to be something to *do*. Something that wasn't just sitting around *waiting*. Carlyle was about to insist upon it when Anna returned, Palmer at her heels.

"He left the house just after four," Palmer said grimly. "Turned off the alarm, then reset it. The footage loses him between the house and the dog barns. There's no sign of him on the barn cameras."

"What about the cabin?"

"The cameras at the cabin are wired. The wires were cut sometime yesterday. But there's no evidence of anyone getting on the property from any of the entrance points."

There was a little chorus of swearing.

"The ranch is just too big to ever be fully secure," Palmer said. "But the fact we've had this kind of trouble multiple times suggests someone knew enough about the setup to circumnavigate it."

"Chessa," Izzy said, her voice wavering.

"But Chessa is dead," Anna pointed out.

"Yes, but she knew the place," Palmer said. Like the rest of them, he glanced at Izzy as if not quite sure how much to say. "She was also allegedly friends with Tripp before he died. He was our ranch hand. He knew the place *and* the security quite well. They might both be dead, but they might have passed along some information to someone who's not."

"We'll start a search party," Jack said. "We know he left on foot. If he got waylaid by someone, the chances are they were on foot as well unless we find tracks. So, we'll split up. In threes. Izzy will stay here with Mary, Dahlia, the baby, some dogs and…" He looked over everyone. "Carlyle."

"Uh-uh. No way."

"You're injured, and we need someone here who's good with a gun."

He was full of it, but as much as she wanted to go look for Cash, Izzy was gripping her hand with such force it almost hurt. The little girl needed her, and Mary might be good at comforting, but Jack was right. Carlyle knew her way around a firearm, and how to protect.

This would be the best thing she could do for Cash, so she nodded.

Jack started deciding groups, but his phone trilled, and he pulled it out of his pocket with a frown. Then swore. Viciously.

But then he looked from Izzy to Mary. "Mary, why don't you take—"

"No," Izzy shouted, jumping to her feet. "What happened? You know something. Don't take me away." She looked up at Carlyle, tears in her eyes but a stubborn set to her mouth. Carlyle wrapped her arm around her shoulders.

"Tell us, Jack."

Jack's mouth hardened, but he nodded. "Someone just texted me a picture of Cash. They're asking for a ransom. So he's fine. He's alive." Carlyle knew Jack said that just for Izzy. "They just want us to pay money to get him back."

"Money, but why?"

Jack didn't answer her. "I'm going to forward Hart the

text. And Brink and have her bring some Sunrise officers out here so we can decide how to proceed."

Carlyle and everyone—but Mary—pushed in close to Jack to see the picture on his screen. How to proceed? Someone had Cash and...

In the picture he was tied up. He had a big bruise on his head and for a moment, a fleeting, terrible moment, she thought he must be dead. But he was scowling. Scowling at the picture-taker.

"They said they're in a hotel in Hardy. They've given me a money drop off point."

"They're not going to give him up," Grant said in a low voice, meant just for the adults.

Carlyle agreed with him, but she wasn't sure what else could be done. They wouldn't just give an address that could be surrounded. "He won't be at the place they're saying. They know you'll go to the cops."

Jack nodded. "No doubt, but we'll have to at least begin to play it their way."

"I want to see," Izzy said, trying to reach up and take the phone from Jack.

"There's nothing to see, sweetie. It's just a picture to show us he's alive and well. They can't get a ransom if he's not. The police will take it from here. It'll be okay."

But Izzy didn't drop her hand. "Let. Me. See."

Carlyle looked from the girl to the picture. It wasn't that bad, and it was clear he was alive. She wasn't sure Izzy needed this stuck in her head, but sometimes knowing was better than the unknown.

"Let her. It'll be better. She won't wonder. She'll know." And they'd find a way to get Cash back here, so this terrible picture wouldn't have to be anyone's last memory. Carlyle swallowed the heavy lump in her throat.

Jack sighed deeply, but then lowered himself into a chair. He motioned Izzy over, then put his arm around her reassuringly as he tipped the phone screen toward her. "He's going to be okay, Izzy. We're going to make sure of it."

Her chin wobbled, and her eyes filled with tears, but then her eyebrows drew together. "That's not a hotel. That's not Hardy."

"What?" Carlyle demanded…along with everyone else.

"Look." Izzy pointed at the bottom edge of the screen, and everyone leaned closer. "That's our kitchen. In the cabin."

Carlyle couldn't figure out what Izzy was pointing at. The picture was mostly just Cash's face, with very little hints at the room around him. She did see a little pink dot behind his ear. Carlyle looked around at the other adults at the table. They were all frowning too.

Izzy pushed Jack's hand out of the way and used her fingers to zoom in on the picture. "There," she said, pointing to the tiny pink dot nearly completely hidden behind Cash's ear. "That's my fairy stained glass thing that hangs in the kitchen window. I *know* it is."

Carlyle let out a breath. It was a stretch, a real reach. She looked behind her, out the kitchen window. The cabin was right there across the yard. She moved over to the window along with everyone else.

"You think they could be in there *now*?" Carlyle asked. She wanted to run across the yard right now and find out, but they all clearly knew on the off chance Cash *was* in there, they had to be very, very careful.

"Why though?" Jack asked. "Why hold him here so close to all of us?"

"Because they told you to go to Hardy," Carlyle said. She didn't want to say the rest in front of Izzy, but maybe it was best if the girl knew. "This isn't about Cash, or not only about him. What has Chessa said she wanted every single time?"

Anna swept a hand over Izzy's hair. "Chessa's dead," she said, once again.

"Sure, but that doesn't mean what she was after just stops. Especially if she was working with people. Butch. Bryan. Whoever. What purpose does it serve to send you off property when we know he's not? To put fewer people on Izzy. Because what were you going to do before the picture, Jack? Have two people and some dogs stay here with Izzy while the rest of you scattered."

Jack said nothing, but she could see a flash of irritation in his eyes. Not because she *was* right, but because he hadn't seen it himself.

"All right. We wait for the police to get here. We surround the cabin. We—"

"That'll take too long and put Cash too much at risk. We have to be sneaky," Carlyle insisted. "We can't go about it the way you normally would. This is about Cash and Izzy, but it's also kind of about you guys as a whole, right? Cash was the one to kick Chessa out, to refuse to pay her, but you all played a role in that. And if Chessa knew you, and passed that along to whoever is part of that, then she knows what you'd do."

"Chessa would have to think about someone besides herself for more than five seconds to know what we'd do," Anna said darkly.

But Jack's gaze never left Carlyle. "What do you suggest then?"

"I think we should give them what they want."

Chapter Eighteen

The response to Carlyle's suggestion was loud. Carlyle let out a sharp whistle to stop it. "Let me finish! Calm down. You guys. Seriously? I am not suggesting we put Izzy in danger. I'm suggesting we lay a trap. Let them think you've gone to Hardy, that we've scattered. Let them think you've handled this in the typical Sheriff Jack Hudson fashion, and then pull the rug out from under them."

"We need to make sure they're still in the cabin first," Grant said. "There's no point to this if they've moved location."

"My phone," Izzy said. "We can track Dad's phone with my phone. But I don't know where Dad puts it at night."

"I do," Mary said, and she hurried out of the kitchen.

Carlyle gave Izzy a squeeze. "Good thinking, kid."

Izzy nodded. She was clutching Carlyle's arm for dear life, but she was holding up. And that was what was holding them all up, Carlyle thought. They couldn't fall apart when they had to come together. They couldn't dissolve when Cash needed them to be strong.

Carlyle looked out the window. She could see just the edge of the cabin. What she really wanted to do was run across the yard, beat down the door and deal with whatever.

But it just didn't make sense. Whoever had Cash had a

plan. Whether they had him in that cabin, in the hotel in Hardy or somewhere completely else, they wanted something. And this would never end until they got to the bottom of what.

And who.

If Chessa was still alive, Carlyle could believe this was all about Izzy. But with her dead, that made less and less sense.

"Did they ever find the stepmother who owned the building?" she asked Jack.

He shook his head. "She's been reported missing by a friend."

"Missing? Not like she took off?"

"It's unclear, but there's some speculation something happened to her, rather than that she's avoiding questions about the explosion."

Carlyle sucked in a breath. Another murder? What could possibly be worth all of this? It didn't add up or make any sense.

Jack's phone rang, making everyone jump. "It's Hart," he muttered, then put the phone to his ear and walked out of the kitchen. Likely so he could speak freely without worrying about Izzy's reaction.

Mary reentered with Izzy's phone. "Here." Mary handed the phone to Izzy. Izzy immediately began to poke away at the screen. She held out the little map that popped up. "He's somewhere close on the property. That means he's in the cabin!"

"He could have left it behind," Anna said gently. Phrasing it in such a way it sounded like that would have been Cash's choice, not his kidnapper's.

"He could have, but I think we know he didn't," Carlyle said, working to keep her words calm. "If Izzy's phone tracks it on the property, and Izzy recognizes the background of that picture, chances are high he is in the cabin. Right *now*. We need to move forward with that plan."

Jack returned. "Hart is on his way. He's going to have a few men on standby at the entrances and exits of the ranch. He didn't think it sounded like a good idea to run code onto the ranch."

"You need to make it look like you're sending out your search teams," Carlyle said. "Mary and I will invite Hart inside when he gets here."

"We're not going anywhere," Jack said resolutely. "If Cash is in the cabin—"

"You don't have to *go*. You just have to make it look like you did. Make it look like Izzy is a sitting duck. But she won't be. Look, we could barge in there and get him out—God knows I'd like to—but we don't know what or who we're dealing with. We have to be more careful. Why not draw them out?"

"Because that takes time, Carlyle." She knew Jack wanted to say more—that it might be time Cash didn't have, but Carlyle refused to believe that. If they were holding him, demanding ransom, they'd keep him alive.

"Cash can handle time," Carlyle insisted. Because he had to. "We have the upper hand if we draw them out. We go in there guns blazing, they do. So we need to do something with the dogs too."

Jack didn't have a response to that. He was scowling, so clearly he didn't agree with her, but maybe he realized they really had no other options.

"Three of you go out together, armed and watchful, and saddle the horses like you're going on a search," Carlyle instructed. "The most likely thing is they're in that cabin, watching. Waiting for us to scatter. We have to act quickly."

There was a pause. Just about everyone in the kitchen—except her brother—looked to Jack. Carlyle wanted to be frustrated, but she understood the family's habitual looking to him to be the leader, to have the final say.

"Walker, Palmer and Grant. Go saddle up four horses. Walk them across the yard to the back of the house. Out of sight of the cabin. We'll tie them up there. Then we'll fan out and form an inner perimeter, out of sight. Any dogs not in a kennel or in the barn, get them there. Carlyle's right. We can't risk them posing a problem."

"Everyone should be armed," Carlyle said. "Every single person." She gave a meaningful jerk of her chin toward Izzy.

This earned Carlyle another glare from Jack. But then he sighed. His telltale sign of giving in. "All right. Palmer?"

"Got it." Palmer disappeared, likely to go gather the firearms in the house from their locked safe.

"I think it should look like as few people are with Izzy as possible, and that Izzy is within as close as reach to the cabin as possible. When Hart gets here, the two of us open the door. Together. And let him in."

"Don't you think we should hide somewhere?" Mary said, worry in every inch of her expression. "We have a great offense—all these people. There's nothing wrong with a little defense."

"We want to draw them out," Carlyle told her, with a gentleness she probably wouldn't have used with anyone else. "They need to get a glimpse of Izzy. They need to think they have this in the bag. The more they think they can easily take her, the better chance we have of doing this cleanly."

Mary didn't say anything to that, but Carlyle watched her reach out for Walker's hand as she placed her other over the slight bump of her stomach.

"You all need to go pretend to search, however Jack

wants that to look. Mary and Dahlia can watch the cabin from upstairs with Caroline. Any kind of binoculars you've got—see if you can get any glimpse inside. Izzy and I stay down here and wait for Hart."

There was another pause. Then Palmer returned with the guns. It was the strangest tableau, everyone standing in the Hudson kitchen, watching as guns were distributed to different people. Palmer hesitated at Izzy, but he handed her the one she'd been practicing with all the same.

"I know you know how to use it, Iz, and we trust you to. But remember, there are a lot of adults around here who can and will handle things. This is just a last resort."

Izzy took the gun and nodded. "I know."

Palmer let out a breath then turned to the remainder of the people in the kitchen. "We should move. The sooner we draw them out, the sooner Cash is safe."

Jack nodded and then everyone began to disperse. Most everyone left out the back door, leaving Carlyle, Izzy, Mary and Dahlia in the kitchen.

Carlyle pulled her phone out of her pocket. "I'm going to start a group call. That way we can all listen and communicate."

"Good idea."

Carlyle started the call on her phone, then shoved it into her pocket on speaker. They all separated, each going to their designated spots. Carlyle took Izzy into the living room, but the girl kept looking over her shoulder.

"Aunt Mary usually isn't scared," Izzy murmured, watching the staircase even though Mary had long disappeared.

Carlyle crouched to be eye level with Izzy and waited for the girl's gaze to meet hers. "There isn't anything wrong with being scared. This is scary. But we're going to fight, even if it's scary."

"I just want my dad to be okay."

"I know. We all do. So, he's going to be. Come on. Let's watch for Hart." She held Izzy's free hand and pulled her over to the big front window. They watched the lane that led up to the house without saying anything.

"I don't want to just sit around waiting, Carlyle," Izzy said, a frustrated and determined look on her face that concerned Carlyle almost as much as Cash being held so close without anyone understanding the situation.

In any other time in her life, Carlyle would have jumped in headfirst, but she was responsible for Izzy. Cash would never forgive her if she messed that up, and Carlyle would never forgive herself. So, for the first time in her life she had to go against her instincts and just stay put.

"I don't either, but sometimes… Man, I learned this one the hard way, but sometimes you've got to let other people help you out. You try to do everything on your own, everyone gets hurt."

Izzy didn't say anything to that, but a little cloud of dust started at the ridge. Then the police car appeared. Carlyle squeezed Izzy's hand. "We've got so much help."

The cruiser pulled to a stop at the front porch and Hart got out. He had a hand on his gun, and it was clear even though he was in detective plain clothes, he was wearing Kevlar underneath.

Carlyle pulled Izzy toward the door. She opened it, and fully stepped out herself. She then pulled Izzy behind her, so hopefully if someone in the cabin was watching they'd catch a glimpse of the little girl and know she was at Carlyle's side.

"Come on in, Hart."

"Where's Jack?" he asked as he followed Carlyle inside.

Carlyle explained her theory on what these people wanted.

She described the Hudson plan of keeping out of sight but close enough to know what was going on. She even explained where everyone in the house was and why she had Izzy with her.

Maybe she hadn't always trusted these cops, but now she had no choice.

"You're going to leave," she told him. "Drive all the way out. Then walk back in. Form an outer perimeter with your guys, and Zeke because he'll be here soon enough. We've got the inner. You start making a tighter and tighter circle, but the main directive is to stay out of sight from the cabin. They'll come out. Likely just one at first, but they'll come out. It's got to be more than one, so you don't want to intercede until we're sure there's no danger to Cash."

"This *is* my investigation."

"And this is my home. And the people I love," Carlyle replied. "My plan's good. The best you're going to get."

Hart glanced down at Izzy, who—to Carlyle's pride—had a lifted-chin, stubbornly defiant expression on her face. She shouldn't be holding a gun, worried about her father's life, but here she was, holding up. Holding true.

"All right. Here." He unhooked a radio from his vest. "You'll be able to hear us communicating with each other. Anything bad goes down inside, you radio out. Just press this button and talk."

Carlyle nodded. It was a good addition to her plan. Not that she was going to admit that to him.

"Anything strikes you as off, you're going to radio us, okay?"

She nodded. "I've got everyone else on a group call in my pocket. We'll do our best to communicate everything to everyone."

"Okay. I'm going to run code off the property, make it look like I'm off to Hardy and the address. Sound good?"

Better than good, but she only nodded. "You trust your guys on the perimeter?"

"With my life," Hart replied.

She hoped to God it wouldn't come to that. She opened the front door once more, letting Hart out then closing the door and locking it.

"Now what?" Izzie asked.

"Now, we have to wait."

Izzie nodded, but she was chewing on her bottom lip. A telltale sign something was bothering her.

Well, why wouldn't she be bothered? Her father was being held against his will in their home.

"It's going to be okay," Carlyle said. She would move hell and earth to make it okay.

Izzy nodded, but when she looked up at Carlyle, the expression in her eyes had Carlyle's stomach sinking.

"Carlyle, I think there's something I need to tell you."

CASH WAS FEELING worse and worse, the headache so bad he wished he could scoop his own brain out to stop the throbbing. Whatever Chessa had shot him up with was a hell of a drug.

Butch had finished with the pantry and was now stationed at the kitchen window. He hid behind the curtain but was watching through a gap. Cash couldn't quite turn his head enough to see out the gap himself, but he kept trying.

Chessa moved around. When it was clear Butch was getting agitated with her, she'd disappear into the living room for a bit, but she always came back. Edgy and pacing.

Cash could see the oven clock and knew it was creeping closer to ten in the morning. He'd been gone too long now. His family would be looking for him. It made no sense why they were keeping him this close to the people who could easily overtake *two* people. Even if they were armed.

"Finally," Butch muttered as the sounds of sirens filled the air.

Cash tried to turn in his seat again, but the bonds were too tight, cutting into his skin. Sirens, yes. But he frowned as the sound went from loud to soft—like the emergency vehicles were leaving the ranch, not coming toward it.

"Go on then," Butch said, jerking his chin at Chessa.

Chessa flashed Cash a self-satisfied grin then slipped out the back door. Cash tried to angle his head so he could see out of the kitchen window, but he couldn't manage it. Where did Chessa think she was going? What had those sirens been? He wanted to demand answers, but even if Butch gave them, Cash could hardly trust them to be true.

"You really think you can trust her to do anything?" he said instead to Butch, because it was a valid enough question. "Particularly when she's on something?"

"Not my rodeo, buddy," Butch muttered.

Cash frowned. Why would Butch pretend like he wasn't involved when it was clear he was? "This is a lot of work and effort if this isn't your rodeo."

"You have no idea the reward," Butch said with a harsh laugh. "Don't worry though. You won't be alive long enough to find out."

But he *was* still alive. For hours on end. Which meant they needed him alive for *something*. "I'm still alive, so…" Cash attempted a shrug despite his bonds. "I guess I'm not too worried about this alleged demise that's coming."

Butch spared him a glance. "For as long as we need you, you'll live. But that isn't much longer."

Chapter Nineteen

Carlyle slowly crouched down and put her hands on Izzy's shoulders. "What do you need to tell me?"

"I… I didn't think it mattered. It was…my little secret. And I would have told everybody, but I didn't think it would—"

"Iz, slow down. Take a breath. Just tell me. Tell me what you've been keeping a secret."

"There's a tunnel."

"A *what*?"

"A tunnel," she repeated, and her eyes were full of tears, her shoulders shaking underneath Carlyle's hands. "Between the cabin and the house. You just have to go into the cellar at the cabin, which is kind of creepy. Then there's this…tunnel. It comes here, through the basement. I don't go there much, but sometimes I just wanted to see… I just wanted to… I don't know. But if Dad is in the cabin, maybe we can get to him through the tunnel. The cellar opens right by the back door."

"Why didn't you tell anyone else?"

For a moment, Izzy didn't say anything. She looked at Carlyle's pocket, where the phone on speaker was, and chewed her bottom lip.

"It was somewhere I could go that nobody knew about. It

was just mine. Just for me and I got to make all the choices there and…"

Carlyle could hear Jack saying something over the speakerphone, but she couldn't focus enough for the words to make sense. She could only try to work through what Izzy was telling her.

A tunnel. To the cabin. To *Cash*.

"Show me," she said to Izzy. Because if she could get to that cabin undetected… They could stop this. "Just show me where the tunnel starts in the basement and—"

"That won't be necessary."

Carlyle jerked Izzy behind her and faced down a woman with a gun. The lady was short, wiry and looked really… rough. The look in her eye was maniacal enough it made Carlyle's whole body run ice-cold. But she held Izzy behind her. No matter what, she'd keep Izzy safe.

"Carlyle," Izzy said in a small voice. "Why did everyone say she was dead?"

Carlyle stared at the woman and realized those blue eyes were familiar because they were the same shade and shape as Izzy's.

Chessa. Not dead, like everyone had said, but here. Alive and with a gun.

"Because Hudsons *lie*, Izabelle," Chessa said, pointing the gun at Carlyle's chest.

"No we don't!" Izzy shouted, trying to come out from behind Carlyle, but Carlyle held her firm. Maybe she didn't know why, but she knew Chessa wanted Izzy, and that sure as hell wasn't going to happen.

"I don't know what you think you're doing, Chessa, but it isn't going to work," Carlyle said, very calmly as she tried to think of what she could do to get Izzy out of here.

Up the stairs. To Mary or Dahlia. She couldn't start shooting until Izzy was safe.

Then Carlyle could do what needed doing. But the staircase was on the other side of Chessa.

Whose finger was curled around the trigger of the gun.

"I don't need you," she said to Carlyle. "I thought Butch should have killed you when he had the chance." So Butch had been the attempted kidnapper. "He's so finicky and weird about things. So mad when I killed that two-bit cop. But he got to off his stepmother, didn't he?" She closed one eye, the gun clearly pointed at Carlyle. She was going to shoot, and Carlyle's only chance at survival was really that she was a bad shot.

Or help.

Because when the gunshot went off, it wasn't Chessa's gun. Or Izzy's or even Carlyle's. Chessa jerked and stumbled face-first onto the ground. Carlyle kept a hard grip on Izzy, keeping her behind her, but moving quickly forward to rip the gun out of Chessa's hand.

She made a low moaning sound as she writhed on the floor, but she didn't get up. Carlyle went ahead and lifted Izzy straight up off the ground and hurried her to the stairs where Dahlia sat on a stair, shaking.

"God, I hate guns," she muttered as Carlyle shoved Izzy at her. Dahlia wrapped her arms around Izzy, even though her arms shook.

"It's okay," Carlyle said. She gave Dahlia's arm a squeeze and looked her straight in the eye. "Hey, you saved the day. Take Izzy upstairs. Be with Mary this time. Lock the door."

"Carlyle—"

But Carlyle wasn't listening. There was a tunnel in the basement. And Cash on the other end.

She looked at Izzy. "Stay safe." Then she ran.

CASH HEARD THE *pop* of what could have only been a gunshot. Somewhere far off, but distinctive enough to know it was a gun. A gun.

Cash looked at Butch, who gave nothing away. He just kept looking out the gap in the curtains.

The minutes that passed were interminable, but as Cash watched Butch, the man's expression began to change. From neutral to more and more irritated. He looked at the clock on the wall more than once.

"Chessa late?" Cash asked.

"Shut up," Butch replied, standing. He walked over to Cash.

Cash didn't know why he didn't stay quiet, didn't know why he was dead set on pissing off the big guy when he was tied to a chair. Maybe Carlyle had gotten to him after all. "Big surprise that Chessa messed everything up."

Butch leaned in and Cash used it as his chance. Maybe he couldn't escape his bonds, but if he could knock Butch out or incapacitate him in some way, then at least there was no threat he'd die.

He used his head to land the hardest blow to Butch's nose that he possibly could. Pain radiated through his own skull on contact, but Butch outright *howled*, and blood spurted from his nose. Butch swore a blue streak as he stumbled back and landed on his butt.

Fury blazed in his expression, and he scrambled over to what Cash had assumed was just a bag of food pilfered from his pantry. But Butch pulled out a gun.

Well, that wasn't good. But he couldn't work up much fear over the radiating pain in his head, the blurred vision. Maybe he'd given himself a concussion? But he was about to get a gunshot wound for the trouble.

"I wouldn't," a female voice said from the kitchen entryway.

Cash could only stare as Carlyle appeared. Butch whirled, but Carlyle was faster. She shot and Butch stumbled back, crashing into the kitchen counter. Carlyle moved over to him while Butch made terrible, pained moans.

She grabbed a knife from the block on the counter and began to saw at the ties around Cash's wrists behind the chair.

"Izzy?" he asked.

"Mary and Dahlia have her."

"They're working for someone. There could be more people out there."

"Cops and your entire family have the whole ranch surrounded." The bonds on his arms fell away and he nearly gasped in relief. "The ransom attempt wasn't the smartest move. No one fell for it. We're safe. She's safe."

She cut the ties at his feet then helped him up. She studied his face. "That's a hell of a knock," she said. He didn't know if she was seeing the mark from hitting Butch, or from earlier, but it didn't matter.

Somehow she was here, and Izzy was safe, and Butch...

Cash wasn't steady on his feet, but he used the counter and the wall to balance as he walked over to where Butch sat.

Butch had pushed himself against the wall. His complexion was gray. Blood poured out of his nose and the bullet wound in his stomach. His eyes were glassy, but they looked from Cash to Carlyle with a kind of resigned hate.

"Who sent you?" Cash demanded. "What do you want with my daughter?"

Butch looked at him, then Carlyle, then at the gun she

held pointed at him. Cash didn't expect an answer. But Butch surprised him.

"Rob Scott."

Cash frowned. "I never had anything to do with Chessa's father. Neither did she."

"Yeah, and that was fine and dandy when she didn't have anything to offer him, but then he got into selling and Chessa helped him out. Got him customers. Worked in a little prostitution ring. She kept talking up how much money she could get for Izzy, how much you'd wronged her. Eventually, he decided to fund her delusion, but she's a loose cannon. I tried to tell him that, but he didn't care if it came with a payday."

"That's a nice story that leaves you completely out of it," Carlyle said while Cash reeled over all of that...truly awful information.

"I don't see anything wrong with wanting to make a profit. I'm not fool enough to use the product like her." He jerked his chin like he was aiming it at Chessa even though she wasn't there. "I'm just muscle. I do what I'm told. And I didn't kill anyone, so what? I'll do a few years' jail time. I ain't worried about it. Probably cut me a deal if I tell them everything. That's the only reason I'm bothering to tell you anything. I don't have any loyalty to Scott."

"Then why work for him?"

"Why not? The money's good, the women are better." He shrugged, even as rivulets of blood flowed out of his nose and stomach. Even as he sat there knowing that even if he survived, he was going to jail. "Better than busting my ass at some minimum-wage job."

Cash didn't see how, but he didn't have to. The sirens were getting closer. "Go open the front door, Car."

Carlyle opened a drawer, pulled out some dish towels. "Push that in there. If he doesn't die, he can testify."

Cash supposed she was right, so he did as he was told. Butch just stared at him. Not with hate, not with interest. Cash stared right back.

"She isn't right, you know," Butch said, then he grunted in pain as Cash pushed harder to stop the bleeding. "You crossed her. She'll never let it go. And now that you got in Rob's way? That's two lunatics with you on their hit list."

Cash supposed, deep down, he'd known that even if he couldn't understand it. In Chessa's mind, he was the villain, and Izzy was hers for the taking. "That a warning, Butch?"

"Nah. Just the truth. I hope it hangs over your head for the rest of your life."

Before Cash could say anything to that, two EMTs rushed in with a stretcher. They pushed Cash out of the way and went to work on Butch, but Carlyle was dragging in another one. "He needs one too," she said, pointing at him.

The EMT walked over to him, took one look at his head and nodded. "Yeah, you've earned yourself a hospital trip."

"Is he good enough to go with me?"

Cash looked behind the EMT to see Detective Hart, but the EMT took him by the chin, moved his head this way and that. Asked him to follow her finger with his eyes. "Yes. But straight to the hospital."

Hart nodded and the EMT released him and strode over to where they were working on Butch. Carlyle led him outside and to the Bent County police cruiser Hart must have been driving.

"I'll go with and—"

Cash cut her off. "Stay here. With Izzy. Please?"

She took a breath, studied him, then nodded. She leaned in, pressed her mouth to his. "Like glue, Cash."

"Thanks."

She helped him into the back of Hart's cruiser, gave his hand one last squeeze, and then didn't just walk off to the cabin, but jogged. He knew she'd keep her promise.

"You up to telling me what happened?" Hart asked as he started the engine.

"Yeah, let's get this over with."

Chapter Twenty

Carlyle woke up feeling fuzzy headed. She was too warm, and under a blanket that smelled like strawberries.

When she blinked her eyes open, she realized she'd fallen asleep with Izzy in Izzy's bed in the kids' room. Izzy was curled up next to her, her fingers wrapped around Carlyle's wrist. For a moment, Carlyle could only watch the girl sleep.

Her heart ached in a million ways, for a hundred reasons. She nearly cried, then and there, but she'd hate to have Izzy wake up to tears.

Because the bad stuff was over now. She didn't know the prognosis on Chessa, or Butch for that matter, but she knew that Izzy was safe. Butch had been happy to rat out who was behind it, and there was no way any of them would be let out of jail for a very long time.

Carlyle would do everything in her power to make certain.

Izzy stirred next to her, yawning as she blinked her eyes open. She met Carlyle's gaze then sat straight up. "Do you think Dad's home?"

Carlyle sat up too and swung her legs over the side. "If he's not, you and I are going to the hospital and demanding to see him."

"Demanding?"

"Oh yeah. Or sneaking into his room. We'll work it out."

Izzy *almost* smiled at that, and they both got up off the bed and walked out into the hallway, the two dogs trailing behind them. Carlyle had no sense of what time it was, or even what day at this point. When they walked down the stairs, Izzy gripped her hand.

They both looked at where Chessa had been, and Carlyle figured she was holding onto Izzy as much as Izzy was holding onto her at this point. They were about to head for the kitchen, but a noise in the living room had them changing course, and as they walked through the hallway, they caught sight of Cash walking in the front door, flanked by Jack and Grant.

"Daddy!" Izzy tried to run over to him, but Carlyle held her firm for a minute.

But Cash nodded, so Carlyle let her go. The little girl raced over to Cash, who knelt to catch her. It was Grant standing behind Cash that clearly kept him from being knocked over by Izzy.

Carlyle stayed where she was, the lump in her throat making it impossible to speak anyway.

"Let's get Cash sitting down," Grant said, helping Cash back up to his feet while Izzy clung to him.

"I'll fill everyone in on the case once we get situated," Jack offered.

There was a bit of a commotion then, people talking at once as the big group of them settled into the living room. Carlyle figured she'd go stand next to Walker, but as she passed the couch where Cash and Izzy were situated, Izzy reached out and gave her arm a tug, so Carlyle had to take a seat right next to her.

With her arms wrapped tight around Cash's arm, she

laid her head on Carlyle's shoulder. Like they were a little unit. Or could be.

"We're questioning Chessa's father," Jack said. "Zeke talked to some of his contacts at a federal agency. It looks like they can build a particularly big case against him— beyond just this. Especially if Butch makes it and testifies, which is looking possible."

"How did Chessa make everyone think she'd been murdered?" Cash asked. His voice was a little raspy, and it looked like he hadn't slept, but he looked...relaxed. Because his daughter was right here.

He moved his arm over Izzy's shoulders, resting his hand on Carlyle's. Carlyle had to blink back the tears stinging her eyes.

Because it was over. Really over. Sure, there were legal steps left. If Chessa survived the gunshot wound, she could still be a threat if she didn't get much jail time. It wasn't some perfect happy ending.

But with so much of the danger neutralized, a happy ending felt like so much possibility Carlyle just wanted to weep.

Jack's expression was grim. "We're still working on identifying the body that was originally ID'd as Chessa's. It looks like they fake-identified the body as Chessa with the help of Ferguson and Rob Scott. Hart's theory is the body is one of her fellow—" Jack's gaze landed on Izzy "—coworkers," he finally said.

So, another prostitute. Carlyle supposed it made sense that Chessa and her father could manipulate things with a woman who worked for them, who they probably knew enough about to hide her identity.

"Butch and Chessa will be under guard at the hospital until they make a full recovery—if they do. Then they'll be transported to jail. Chessa's awake and eager to turn

on everyone. The information Butch gave you corrobo-
rates much of what Chessa said, and Chessa claims Butch
killed his stepmother. Police are looking into that too, but
even without full cooperation, they'll all be on the hook for
first-degree murder. They'll be locked up for a long while."

"What about this tunnel?" Cash asked.

"As far as we can tell, they were old cellars that were
connected," Jack said. "Old enough I'm not even sure our
parents knew about them. They were sealed off, kind of,
it looks like, until..."

"I found the one in the cabin when I was mad one day,"
Izzy said, looking at her lap. "Messing around in the cellar because Dad told me not to. Then I found the tunnel
entrance and it was like a book, and I was mad, so I kept
it a secret. Then it just became this...thing I did whenever
I was mad. Whenever everyone was talking about stuff or
doing stuff they were hiding from me. I didn't unseal the
other side though. I tried, but I couldn't do it." She looked
up at Jack, like she was desperate for him to believe her.

"No, that definitely looked more recent. I think the kidnapping attempt might have been a distraction in more ways
than one. It's possible Chessa and Butch have been hiding
out in the cabin since after that night."

Carlyle absorbed that like a blow. Painful, but what could
you do? It was over, and they'd survived.

"I'm sorry," Izzy said, her voice so small it was a wonder anyone but Carlyle and Cash heard her. "I didn't tell
anyone because... I just wanted to feel like... I just wanted
to have something nobody knew about. That no one could
protect me from. I'm sorry..."

"I'm sorry too, Iz," Cash said, pulling her close. "Sorry
you felt like you needed that."

Izzy nodded and snuggled into him. He glanced at Carlyle over Izzy's head and smiled. "We'll all get a little better at…talking to each other instead of trying to save each other, all on our own. Day by day."

Carlyle managed to smile back, even though she was overwhelmed with too many emotions to wade through. "Yeah." Because that was life. Day by day. Doing their best to do a little better. And she'd finally found a really good place to make her home, and good people to expand her family.

Danger or no, she was exactly where she wanted to be with the people she wanted to be with—all who'd worked together to keep each other safe and sound, no matter what threats were hurled at them.

What more could anyone ask for?

AFTER A FEW DAYS, Cash couldn't say he felt back to one hundred percent, but he felt more in control of his body. Felt like he'd dealt with what had happened, mostly.

Carlyle had handled working with the dogs for the past few days, with only moderate supervision from him as everyone was always fussing at him to rest. Then they ate their family dinner, put Izzy to bed together and came out onto the porch to watch the sunset, with Swiftie never leaving Carlyle's side for long.

It was a nice little routine. Rocking on the porch swing, her head in his lap as night slowly crept over the world.

Tonight, he was staring at his cabin. The place he'd raised his daughter, and then been held against his will.

"I don't think I can ever live there again." He twisted a lock of Carlyle's hair around his finger.

"So why not bulldoze it and start over?"

"Seems like a waste of a house."

"Sounds therapeutic to me. We can take a sledgehammer to it together. Have a destruction party."

Cash laughed, even though it hurt his head a little. "I'll keep that in mind."

And it was amazing, really. How she made everything feel infinitely possible. All those doors he'd closed and locked on himself, she'd busted open just by being her.

So, he figured tonight was as good a night as any. "You know I'm in love with you, right?"

She didn't say anything at first, but she did smile up at him. That brash, cocky smile that had first made her seem like some foreign beacon of light he couldn't resist.

"Yeah, I figured as much."

"You going to admit you're in love with me yet?"

She made a considering noise. "What's in it for me if I do?"

"Good question."

"I guess a hot guy in my bed," she said thoughtfully, as though she were ticking off points on a list.

He gave her a disapproving look. "Or my bed."

"And you're pretty decent when it comes to housework. That's a plus." She sat up and squinted out at the sunset as if considering.

He shook his head. "If you say so."

"And I like a man who can be a good dad to his daughter. If you couldn't, no amount of hotness could make up for it."

"You've got quite the criteria there."

"And the dogs. They can sense evil, so since they love you, you must not be evil."

"I'm glad the dogs are what convinced you of that."

She laughed then looked at him, her blue-gray eyes twinkling with mischief. "You're a pretty good package, Cash."

"Great," he muttered, because he knew she was messing with him, and he knew she got a kick out of it when he acted messed with.

She leaned her head on his shoulder and sighed. "I love you, Cash."

They watched the sun slip behind the horizon, not thinking about how everything would be happy and easy from here on out, but that no matter what was thrown at them, they'd always have that love.

* * * * *